ALSO BY MICHELE YOUNG-STONE

Above Us Only Sky
The Handbook for Lightning Strike Survivors

lost
in the
beehive

A NOVEL

michele young-stone

Simon & Schuster Paperbacks

New York   London   Toronto   Sydney   New Delhi

Simon & Schuster Paperbacks
An Imprint of Simon & Schuster, Inc.
1230 Avenue of the Americas
New York, NY 10020

First Simon & Schuster trade paperback edition April 2018

SIMON & SCHUSTER PAPERBACKS and colophon are registered trademarks of Simon & Schuster, Inc.

For information about special discounts for bulk purchases, please contact Simon & Schuster Special Sales at 1-866-506-1949 or business@simonandschuster.com.

The Simon & Schuster Speakers Bureau can bring authors to your live event. For more information or to book an event, contact the Simon & Schuster Speakers Bureau at 1-866-248-3049 or visit our website at www.simonspeakers.com.

Interior design by Carly Loman

Manufactured in the United States of America

1   3   5   7   9   10   8   6   4   2

Library of Congress Cataloging-in-Publication Data
Names: Young-Stone, Michele, author.
Title: Lost in the beehive : a novel / Michele Young-Stone.
Description: New York : Simon & Schuster, 2018.
Identifiers: LCCN 2017029177 | ISBN 9781451657647 (softcover)
Subjects: | BISAC: FICTION / Literary. | FICTION / Coming of Age. |
FICTION /
General. | GSAFD: Bildungsromans. | Love stories.
Classification: LCC PS3625.O975 L67 2018 | DDC 813/.6—dc23
LC record available at https://lccn.loc.gov/2017029177

ISBN 978-1-4516-5764-7
ISBN 978-1-4516-5766-1 (ebook)

For Merritt Daniel McGovern Stone

Like George, you lassoed the moon

The bee is a miraculous creature:
it defies the laws of gravity and aerodynamics,
carrying three times its own body weight,
flapping its wings over two hundred beats per
  second.
It is a creature not just of this world, but of the
  world to come.
Pay attention to the bees. You might learn
  something.

—MADAME ZELDA

part one

The world breaks everyone, and afterward many are strong at the broken places.

—Ernest Hemingway, *A Farewell to Arms*

1

ONE OF US WAS GOING to die. I watched the bees fly erratically along the ceiling. They hovered where the plaster hung in sheets. He was bearing down, his thighs straddling my waist, his hands at my throat, the back of my head pounding the bathroom tile. I heard Zelda scream, "Mommy!" but I couldn't answer. I heard the hum of bees, the noise growing louder. I squirmed and kicked as he bore down. With my left hand, I dug at the cracked tile, feeling for a shard, something to fight back.

Zelda shouted, "Get off Mommy!"

The bees swarmed above his head while I clawed the floor. I felt a piece break free in my hand, my head whacking the floor once more, the light disappearing, something warm on my cheek. The black-and-white basket-weave tiles were cracking open, and I was falling between them. Then, I heard a familiar voice, one I hadn't heard since I was just a kid. It was my very own Peter Pan, the boy who wouldn't grow up. He said, "I've got you, Gloria. I've always got you."

2

PETER PAN'S REAL NAME WAS Sheffield Schoeffler. I met him my first week at the Belmont Institute. The year was 1965. I remember that on the drive to the institute, my mother leaned over the seat back in her cat-eye sunglasses. "You'll get better at this place. They're going to make you like everybody else." She reached out to touch my hand, and I thought about that movie *Invasion of the Body Snatchers*. I'd never wanted to be like everybody else.

My father said, "This is it." I nearly said, *Let's turn around. I don't want to do this,* but everyone, especially my mother, thought that the Belmont Institute was a good idea.

I wasn't optimistic. The institute, with its spiked gate, winding black drive, and stone fortress, replete with towers and a parapet, looked like something out of a Vincent Price horror movie.

I remember that the day was gray, the rain falling in spurts, the leaves on the pin oaks the color of marigolds and rust. Father pulled our car beneath the building's awning, and before he cut the engine, Dr. Belmont emerged between two iron doors. He was a short man, wearing wire spectacles that matched his thick silvery hair. He wore an oxford dress shirt, the sleeves rolled up, and a navy-blue tie. His slacks and shoes were brown.

He shook my parents' hands, telling them that they'd made a wise decision. "Gloria will get the best care here." He patted my father's back. "Our success rate is unmatched." Then, Dr. Belmont came toward me, his beady eyes magnified within the silver frames. He put his hand under my chin, raising my face to meet his. I wore a pink baseball cap, a gift from my neighbor Gwen Babineaux. He pulled it off my head. "She won't be needing this here." He handed it to my mother.

Then, he clapped his hands together. "Everything's in order. We've got your papers, and you have the information packet. Correct?"

My mother said, "Can we see her room?"

"No. Unfortunately not." He shook his head. "We don't allow family into the facility. It's part of the recovery process. That's covered in the brochure and the contract you signed."

My mother nodded. Then, she started to cry, dabbing her eyes with her white-gloved hands. Dr. Belmont pulled a handkerchief from his back pocket. "We'll take good care of her."

I pushed at the iron door. I was ready to go, get it over with already.

"Gloria," my dad called, but I kept pushing. This was what everyone wanted. This was what I'd agreed to. So be it. Dr. Belmont came up behind me. "All right, then. We're eager to get started." We passed through the door, and the world I knew was gone.

Dr. Belmont put his hand at the small of my back and led me into a great hall. In the center of the room, there was a four-sided desk where his assistant, Mrs. Winningham, sat. He introduced us. She had long black hair and false eyelashes. "She knows most anything you'll need to know while you're here," he said.

I said, "Nice to meet you."

"We'll see about that." She laughed. "I'm only teasing."

"How long will I be here?"

Dr. Belmont said, "You'll be with us until you're cured. It's in the contract your parents signed."

Mrs. Winningham said, "Everyone responds differently to treatment. There's no magic number. It depends on how hard you're willing to work. Like Dr. Belmont said."

"I'll leave you to it, Mrs. Winningham." As Dr. Belmont walked away, he whistled a show tune that echoed in the great hall.

Mrs. Winningham said, "This way, Gloria. I'll show you to your room." I trailed her up a marble staircase with an ornately carved wooden banister, down a narrow hallway, and onto a compact elevator. The iron door clanked as she latched it. I said, "I forgot my suitcase."

"You didn't forget it. I have it. I'll be going through it checking for contraband. You wouldn't believe the items some people bring here."

The elevator rattled as we went up two flights. On the landing, there was a brass plaque set in the marble floor. Oxidized a bluish green, it read, *Hard work is the path to righteousness.* Already, I didn't like the Belmont Institute.

The ceiling was low and the landing was dimly lit. I followed Mrs. Winningham down another narrow hall, past a dozen beige doors.

"What are all these rooms?"

"They're for patients like yourself. Please keep up." I followed her down another hallway. "Here we are." She pulled a ring of keys from her pocket and unlocked my door. "It's imperative that you keep your door shut and stay in your room unless accompanied by myself, an assistant, or one of the doctors. Do you understand?"

"Yes, ma'am." I looked around. The room was a cell: a metal shelf was attached to a stone wall. There was a thin mattress, a small bedside table, and a window no bigger than my hand. I'd really messed up. I never should've agreed to come here. "When will I get my suitcase?"

"Later today."

"What am I supposed to do?"

"Rest." She pulled my door shut. I sat on the mattress and waited for my suitcase. The window was more prism than clear glass. Would Mrs. Winningham bring sheets? I wondered. What was Isabel doing? Had my parents gotten home yet? How long would I be here? When I could see darkness through the prism, I lay back staring at the spackled ceiling, counting the peaks and valleys, craving my suitcase, my books and journals, the things that kept me sane.

At some point during the night, Mrs. Winningham came to my room. "Here we are," she said.

"What time is it?"

"I'm not sure."

My suitcase felt lighter. "You must know the time," I said.

"Maybe seven. I'm not sure."

"It seems later." I unzipped my case. "Where are my books?"

"Those books were inappropriate."

"What about my journals?"

"I read them, Gloria. Not good, sweetheart. You can share your secrets with your counselor now. Your notebooks were filled with the kinds of thoughts you're here to overcome."

"Those were my personal journals." I felt sick to my stomach. "Can I call my parents?"

"I'm afraid not."

"Please."

"No."

"Can I see Dr. Belmont?"

"No. Not today." I stepped toward Mrs. Winningham,

thinking I could push past her, find my way out of this maze down to the great hall and telephone my parents. If I explained how this place was, they'd come for me, but then a hulking woman with a square face came instead. She towered over Mrs. Winningham. "This is Miss Rondell. She keeps an eye on your floor." Mrs. Winningham addressed the giantess. "Gloria is having a hard time with our rules. She only just arrived today, so she doesn't understand how the mind must be cleansed before it can be restored to its original state."

Miss Rondell nodded.

"I just want to call my parents."

Mrs. Winningham smiled. "You don't realize it now, but we're helping you. You're being saved."

I felt defeated. "I'm thirsty. May I please have a glass of water?"

"Miss Rondell will get you a glass of water. You get some rest, and someone will meet with you tomorrow."

"Can I have something to read?"

"Of course. Miss Rondell will get you something." The giantess wandered off. Mrs. Winningham followed.

My water never came. I didn't sleep. I thought about Isabel. I never stopped thinking about her. She was the reason I was here. I'd fallen in love, and everyone said that it was wrong, a sin, an illness even. I guess I kind of believed them. If there was a cure for the way I felt, I was willing to swallow that pill, get her out of my head for good, but lying on my mat all alone, I couldn't help imagining her silky hair, the last time I'd run my fingers through it, and her tan breasts, her tiny brown nipples, how they'd felt pressed against mine. I rolled over, my hand between my legs.

In the morning, Miss Rondell came to my room.

"I never got my water. I never got anything to read."

"Come with me," she said.

I followed her to the dining hall. There were three rectangular tables, two crowded with young people about my age. They sat boy, girl, boy, girl. Miss Rondell led me to the third table, which was empty. "Stay here," she said, "and I'll get your tray."

"Can I call my parents?"

She didn't answer. I noticed that there were a lot more boys than girls at Belmont. I tried making eye contact, tried smiling at a couple of them, but it was like I was invisible.

"No one is going to talk to you," Miss Rondell said, dropping my tray in front of me. "If you talk to them, you'll get them in trouble, so it's best to keep your eyes on your tray."

"Why?"

Miss Rondell left without a word. I looked enviously at the other two tables, then back at my tray. My eggs were gray, my toast was burned, and my orange juice was warm. I pushed the tray away, then made my way to the serving line. I was still thirsty. A middle-aged woman in a hairnet said, "What do you need, sweetheart?"

"Just a glass of water, please."

"Just a sec." She brought me a glass, and I drank it down.

"May I have another, please?"

She brought me another, and I quaffed it. "May I please have another?"

"You sure are thirsty."

"I got here yesterday and they wouldn't even bring me a glass of water."

She shrugged. I drank a fourth glass before returning to my table. A blond-headed boy at table two smiled at me, breaking the rules. I smiled back. Then, I managed to swallow my toast. The teenagers' voices rose and fell, but as soon as Mrs. Winningham entered the cafeteria, the room went silent. With her black eyes, she was like some demon. She held a clipboard at her chest, walking the perimeters of the three tables, jotting down notes. When she left, the talking resumed.

Miss Rondell came back, and I didn't bother asking any questions. I followed her to an institutional bathroom where she handed me a toothbrush, a tube of toothpaste, and a bar of soap. "I'll wait outside," she said. "There's a towel and robe hanging inside the shower stall."

There were no mirrors. I brushed my teeth and took a shower. The water smelled of rust, and there were red rings around the metal grating. The robe had pockets but no tie. I slid my toothpaste and toothbrush in the right pocket and left the soap in the bathroom. My feet were bare. Miss Rondell looked down and said, "I forgot your slippers."

"It's all right." My feet actually felt good against the cold floor.

As soon as we were back at my room, she pulled the door shut. No good-bye. Nothing. There was now a plastic pitcher of water by my bed (they must've heard how thirsty I was), and beside it, the King James Bible and a stack of pamphlets. My reading material . . . Of course. I flipped through the little books: *What's Wrong with Me?*, *How Can I Know God?*, and *Taking the First Steps*. I started with *What's Wrong with Me?* Why not?

> *Homosexuality is a mental illness, a sexual perversion stemming from early childhood trauma. There is nothing wrong with you. There is something wrong with your brain. You are mentally ill.*

I set the pamphlet down, picking up another one. Basically, they all said the same thing. I was a sick pervert. I didn't really feel like a sicko. I felt like a girl who'd been dumped, who'd had her heart trampled. I wanted a cure for that.

I picked up the Bible, flipped to the bookmarked pages, to Leviticus 20:13: *If a man also lie with mankind, as he lieth with a woman, both of them have committed an abomination: they shall surely be put to death*; then I turned to Romans 1:26–27 and read about God giving women up to vile affections. The Bible was talking about me: *for even the women did change the natural use into that which is against nature.* I rolled my eyes. I'd been raised in the Catholic church. I knew the Bible. I knew what I was doing: sinning and going to Hell. I had no illusions about any of it. Yes, absolutely, Hell for her. Since setting eyes on Isabel, eternal damnation had been something I was willing to accept.

3

ON DAY FOUR, I MET the blond boy, Sheffield Schoeffler, who'd broken the rules by smiling at me in the cafeteria. Mrs. Winningham escorted me to the great hall and lined me up alphabetically with the others. It was one of the few times in my life where I was beside an *S* (a Schoeffler) and not sandwiched between a Racine and a Russo. Sheffield was tall and thin. I'd been alone and silent for so long that when I spoke, the words sounded funny. First I said, "Thanks for smiling." When he didn't say anything, I said, "I just want to go home."

He looked at me. "I get it, Blondie. We all want to go home." He crossed his arms. "They won't let you go home. It's in the contract. I'm sure you've heard about the contract." His eyes were blue-gray and seemed to alternate between the two hues as he spoke. I was staring at them. He had an oval face and pink lips. He continued, "I know it's hard when you first get here, and they won't let you talk to anybody, but I promise that later, you'll wish you could keep quiet. Just wait."

Dr. Belmont approached us in his wire-rimmed spectacles. "Mr. Schoeffler," he said, "you've come back to us, and we are sorely glad for it. Please do us the honor of sharing what you needed to say to Miss Ricci that was so important that you had to interrupt morning prayers."

Sheffield cleared his throat. "Well, I was only telling her that she'll really like it here. I liked it so much, I've returned."

Dr. Belmont said, "I'm not going to have any trouble with you, am I?"

Sheffield didn't answer.

Dr. Belmont clamped onto Sheffield's jaw, holding it between his thumb and forefinger, the soft white side of his forearm exposed. "I'm not going to have any trouble with you, am I?" he repeated. A smirk crept across Sheffield's face as a blue vein appeared on Dr. Belmont's arm. They stared at each other until Dr. Belmont removed his hand and turned to me. "Welcome, Gloria." He hadn't spoken to me since the day I'd arrived, since handing me over to Mrs. Winningham. I kneaded the side seams of my blue dress.

"Good morning," I said.

"I'm sorry that you have the bad luck of alphabetically preceding Mr. Schoeffler here."

"Thank you." I didn't know what to say.

"Let us bow our heads and pray. Nothing is possible without the Lord's grace. Heavenly Father, you sacrificed your only son so that we might be saved. Today, I ask that you forgive me of my sin." Dr. Belmont walked down the line of teenagers, stopping every now and again to place his right hand on a person's head or lift a chin. "Jesus loves you." I started crying, not because of Jesus, but because of the way Dr. Belmont had grabbed Sheffield. Because I was lonely, because I missed my home, my bed. Everything.

Dr. Belmont said, "Now, I want each of you to take as much time as you need and confess your own sin to the Lord."

Sheffield said, "Well, I couldn't help myself. Really, I couldn't stop myself. He was so handsome."

"Silently!" Dr. Belmont bellowed, his face flush.

Sheffield stifled a laugh while I prayed, my lips moving, hoping Dr. Belmont would notice, hoping he'd believe that I wanted to be cleansed or whatever it was I had to do.

Dr. Belmont said, "I know you are with me, Lord." He walked up and down the line, hands clasped behind his back. "I am going to honor you in my life every day with every breath." Then, he broke into the Lord's Prayer, and everyone joined in because the Lord's Prayer was like the Pledge of Allegiance. No one had to think about its meaning.

After prayers, Dr. Belmont dismissed us to begin our daily routine. I turned to follow Miss Rondell, and Sheffield took hold of my pinky and squeezed. "You're going to be all right." I squeezed back.

I reported to art therapy at nine; to my counselor, Mrs. Dupree, at ten thirty; and at noon, I went to lunch in the dining hall. I was now allowed to talk quietly with the others, but the conversations felt stilted. Everyone at Belmont was working hard to get out of the institute, and there was a real sense that anything anyone said might later be used against them—reported to Dr. Belmont, Mrs. Winningham, or one of the counselors. Everyone was on guard except for Sheffield Schoeffler, who antagonized Dr. Belmont whenever he had the chance.

At twelve forty-five, I had physical education, and from two to four, I had reading and mathematics. Prayers and lectures lasted from four to six. Then, we had dinner. The next day was the same. As was every day that followed, except Friday. Fridays were special. At seven o'clock, there was a social in the ballroom on the first floor. It was a grand, romantic space with a vaulted ceiling and crystal chandelier. Underfoot, there was a tile mosaic of a country scene with girls in bustles and hats, a horse pulling a cart. I walked back and forth, imagining myself in the cart leaving Belmont.

Against the far wall, there was a long table covered with an embroidered tablecloth, a punch bowl with crystal glasses hanging from the rim, and a plate of sugar cookies. On that first Friday, I stood against the wall, holding a glass of punch. Sheffield Schoeffler approached, offering me a cookie.

"Thank you."

"Sure," he said. "They're free and everything."

I smiled.

He stood beside me, his back against the wall. "What's your name? I got the Ricci part. It precedes Schoeffler."

I nibbled the cookie, watching the boys and girls dance stiffly across the tiles. "Gloria."

"Mine's Sheffield, but you can call me Sheff."

The last thing I needed, and I knew it, was an alliance with a troublemaker. Then again, he was the only one with any chutzpah, who didn't seem defeated at square one. I guess I should've known: I've always been attracted to chutzpah.

"So, what's your story?" he asked. "What brings you here?"

"I don't have a story."

"Me either. That's cool. No one here has a story. It's just a fun place to be."

I turned to face him. "I'd rather not say. That's all. I'm just trying to get along and get out of here."

He seemed to consider what I'd said. "Well, I'll tell you mine."

I shrugged. "If you want."

"You don't have to beg . . ."

I smiled.

"Here goes: I was a pretentious faggot menace. I came here last year, and they cured me of pretentiousness, but not the faggot-menace bit, and apparently that's the real problem. Who knew?"

I cracked up, spraying cookie crumbs.

"Okay, now it's your turn."

I sipped my punch before beginning, "First, I shouldn't be here. If they'd let me call my parents, I know that they'd come get me. I wasn't forced to come here. I actually agreed to come here."

"So you're certifiably insane."

"Basically."

"They won't," he said, "let you call your parents. I'm sorry. But it's nice to know that if you did call them, they'd come get you, but they won't let you call." He paused. "My parents sent me here. If they could, they'd keep me here forever. My pop thinks I'm some kind of karmic payback for all the fags he terrorized at university. My mother can't stand me."

"That's awful."

Sheff shrugged. "So, why in the world did you agree to come here, Gloria Ricci?"

"I'm a lesbian, I guess."

"You guess. You're not sure."

"I mean, I just fell in love. But she doesn't love me." I tipped my head back. "I'm not going to cry."

He looked genuinely sad. "Don't cry. It's best to save the boohooing for when you repent. Then, your counselor will really want to see you fall apart. Trust me on this one." Sheff sipped his punch. "My pop says he'll have this place burned to the ground if they don't fix me. He's a steel man. He owns the company and oversees the factory operations. He expects everyone to fall in line, especially me."

"My dad works for the phone company."

"Is your dad awful?"

"He means well," I said.

"My parents are complete terrors. The worst. They've already picked out the girl I'm supposed to marry. Can you imagine? It's medieval. Her name is Buttercup Hepburn. We're supposed to join two great families together."

"Like a dynasty or something."

"I guess, but I'm not marrying Buttercup Hepburn. When I get out of here, I'm going to Chelsea. There's a boy there waiting for me. He looks like Sal Mineo."

"I love Sal Mineo. *Rebel Without a Cause* is one of my favorite movies."

"You'll have to get your own Sal Mineo. This one's mine." He smiled. His eyes were tiny sapphires under the chandelier light.

"Are you in love with him?"

"I don't know what that is."

"Very funny."

"I'm serious." He handed me a napkin and touched around his mouth to let me know that I had a red-punch mustache. "I've never been in love. I've been in lust, but not love." We went to a line of chairs running the length of the wall. Sheff said, "Tell me about your great love, but only if you can do it without crying."

"She went home to Virginia. She's getting married." I felt the tears pooling.

"Married. Really? How old is she?"

"Almost seventeen."

"And she's getting married?"

"Next year. She said that I was just a summer fling, a phase. She wrote me a letter. She said that we weren't real, and she said that she was sorry if I thought otherwise." I wiped the tears from my cheeks.

"What a bitch."

We sat there in silence. After a moment, he turned to me. "Do you want to dance?"

"I'm not very good."

"We're basically in prison," he said. "I'm not exactly picky when it comes to dance partners."

He was such a show-off, displaying an amalgamation of dance steps, a regular Gene Kelly with his fancy footwork. I expected him to dance up the wall, but then he settled down, taking my hand and pulling me close. As we moved across the floor, he told me about his family's cook, Gabby. "She's been with us since I was two." He spun me, tossing one hand in the air. "Added flair," he noted before continuing. "She's the one who first taught me to dance and to cook. She doesn't even care that I'm gay."

I thought of my neighbor Gwen Babineaux. When my mother had been absent, she'd been there for me. I told Sheff about Gwen, how she'd cooked for me and my dad. "She never taught me to dance, but I know she would've if I'd asked." Sheff and I danced and talked until the social ended at ten o'clock. "Sit with me at dinner tomorrow," he said.

"Absolutely."

When I returned to my room, moonlight filled the prism window. Soon, it would disappear, and it would be dark again. I rolled over to face the wall, remembering Isabel, how our last night together had ended with her standing on her aunt's front porch while I was guided into the back seat of a police car.

4

AT DINNER THE NEXT NIGHT, I sat beside Sheff. He was playing with his food. Outside, it began to rain, and the drops pattered against the window. Sheff turned to me. "I've been thinking. I might try aversion therapy."

"What's that?"

"I don't know exactly, but they say it works." He rearranged his green beans, calling them grass. "I can't be who I am and get out of this place. Dr. Belmont guarantees that this therapy works, so if I do it, my dad will think I've changed."

"Do you want to change? Do you want to go with girls? Do you want to be what your pop wants you to be?" I put a green bean above my lip, pretending it was a mustache, wanting to see him smile.

"No. Of course not. I just want to be left alone. I want to get out of here, go to Chelsea, find Sal Mineo."

"I shouldn't have come here," I said. "They're not helping me."

"They don't help anyone."

With two green beans, I made an *X* on my forehead.

"You should come to Chelsea," he said. "When we get out of here, we should meet there."

"We should." I paused. "We will."

But I never thought we would. Not really.

At our next Friday night social, Sheff took my hand and led me to the darkest corner of the ballroom. He pulled me down where we wouldn't be seen by the chaperones. "It was the first baseman, Chip Lightner," he began. I sat with my knees to the side while Sheff crouched.

"Who's Chip Lightner?"

"The reason I'm back here again. Dr. Belmont never tires of hearing this story. He's the real pervert. Not us." Sheff took a deep breath. "I never showered with the other guys at school. I always waited. I didn't care if I was late to class. . . . I just felt weird being there with the others because everybody knew that I liked boys. I tried to be invisible, keep my nose clean, but then one day, I go to take a shower after I think everybody's gone, but Chip's there in the locker room. 'I was waiting for you,' he says. And I'm not stupid. I was waiting for a bunch of guys to jump out and kick my ass, but it didn't go that way. Chip put his hands on my waist." Sheff swallowed hard, then dropped his head before looking up at me, his eyes gray. "Chip started trying to unzip my pants, and I'm telling him to leave me alone. I wanted to get out of there. Just the same, I was rock hard." Sheff shook his head. "If I could take that blow job back, I fucking would. I'd take it back in a second . . . Of course, the football coach walked in. Mind you, Chip's the one on his knees, but the coach yells for me to get away from him like it's all me, all my fault." Sheff leaned forward, pretending to take a bow. "Yes, yes, thank you. No need for a standing ovation. I'm the great faggot menace, so it was all my doing. I forced my dick into the baseball player's mouth. Good show, Mr. Schoeffler." Then, he seemed to crumble. He pulled his legs to his chest, and I heard him sniffling. He was breaking his own rule. He was about to cry.

I said, "You're a threat to baseball players everywhere. No wonder they locked you up."

"I lied to you before," he whispered. "If I could get fixed, if I could really get fixed and be straight, I would. I'd do it in a minute. It would just make everything easier."

"Don't say that."

"Why?"

I put my arms around his neck. "You wouldn't be you."

He smiled faintly. "I like your hair." He reached for one of my curls and twisted it around his finger.

"And at least you gave up pretense. You can't forget that. That's a big deal."

We sat across from each other, my curls wrapped in his pointer fingers. We were simpatico. Sheff took a deep breath. "After the coach went to see my pop, Pop asked me, 'Why do you do this?' and I said, 'Because you expect it from me.' Then, Pop hauled off and punched me in the jaw. I wasn't going to fight him about going back to Belmont. I just didn't have it in me. Later, I told him I was sorry, that I was going to do better, but he didn't want to hear it."

"I'm sorry," I said.

"It's your turn. Tell me a story."

I unwound my hair from his fingers, and taking his hands in mine, we scooted so that our backs were against the wall, our legs side by side. My yellow strappy heels in line beside his black oxfords. "My first kiss was with a girl named Amelia. She and I went to elementary school together."

"Sounds terribly inappropriate."

I smiled. "It wasn't. Not really. At lunch, Amelia would sit with her leg pressed to mine. In class, she scooted her desk closer to mine. She made it a good two feet before Sister Teresa warned her to retreat. 'We don't move our desks, Amelia,' she scolded, all nunlike, making a big show, thwacking her yardstick on Amelia's desk. I remember that Amelia burst into tears, but she refused to move her desk back. The nuns moved the desk with her sitting in it." I laughed.

"In fifth grade, she chased me to a big oak on the edge of

the playground and we kissed. It was the most natural thing. We kissed again. Then she ran off. It was innocent, but I really liked her. Maybe that's when I first knew I liked girls, liked kissing them. You know . . . Then, on the last day of sixth grade, Amelia came up to me on the playground and said she'd be going to a different school for seventh grade. She said, 'You won't see me again.' I asked her if she was moving, and she said no, that she was just changing schools, so I asked why, and I remember her saying, 'Because I'm not like everybody else.'

"I pursued it. 'What do you mean?'

"She said, 'You're not the first girl I've kissed. I keep getting caught.' I never saw her again. I've always wondered if the next school in the next town or wherever fixed her, made her like everybody else. I wish that I'd said something like, 'I'm not like everybody else either,' but I think that I acted like it was no big deal."

"And you're pining over some girl named Isabel? Who cares about Isabel? Sounds like you need to find this Amelia."

"You're right." I held back tears.

Sheff talked about his Gabby. "When I was little and I had a nightmare or got scared, she'd let me sleep with her. When I was four or five, I had a bad dream and tried climbing in bed with my parents, but my mother woke and said, 'What are you doing in here?' I told her I'd had a bad dream, and she said, 'You're not a baby. Go back to your own bed.'" He paused. "Obviously, she's a really swell mother. So, I started going to

Gabby's room. She'd make me a glass of warm milk, read a story, tuck me in beside her. She's always been good to me."

"I get it, how important it is to have somebody like that. My mom and I used to be close." I remembered the years before the twins died, how when the weather was warm we would play in the backyard. She'd pretend to eat the mud pies I made. She brought out wooden spoons, bowls and pots, and while I ran the hose, slinging mud, she let me wear her favorite apron. Twice a week, I helped her with the laundry, handing her wet clothes from the basket while she pinned them to the line. I would reach as high as I could, saying, "I'm almost as tall as you," and she'd tousle my hair. She was my favorite person until I wasn't hers.

"What happened?" Sheff asked.

"She got depressed." I heard the jingle of keys and looked up to see the janitor, Mr. Weathers, pushing his mop. Then, Mrs. Winningham, dark-eyed demon, was on his heels. "What are you two doing? The dance is over. You're not supposed to be here."

As we parted, Sheff squeezed my pinky. "See you tomorrow."

Yes. Tomorrow. I had something to look forward to.

5

MRS. DUPREE, MY COUNSELOR, HAD patchwork scars up
and down her arms, but she kept them hidden beneath flouncy
sleeves that draped over her wrists. She had light brown hair
and brown eyes. Aside from her scars, there was nothing striking about her. She told me that she'd been a member of the
Pentecostal Holiness Church before being called to work with
Dr. Belmont, as if the Belmont Institute were a religious order.
We met daily. She set a timer for ninety minutes. It ticked away
while I sat in a hard-back chair, a mammoth desk between us.
There were no bathroom breaks except for emergencies. During every session, I was told that the only way to acknowledge
and accept my sin was to relive the experience. With each detail I revealed, Mrs. Dupree's words became more volatile, and
I became more vulnerable: "Do you think that lying naked

with another girl is acceptable in the eyes of God? It's not," she assured me. "A man lies with a woman to bear fruit. Do you want to be filthy in the eyes of God?" I knew that my God and Anna Dupree's god were not the same.

I still believed in God then.

For every good memory I relayed, she explained that Isabel and I were not in our right minds. What existed between us was not love. "Do you think Isabel Sullivan cares about you? Do you think she loved you? Because she didn't. You were the devil's instrument." She continued, "Do you know that God so loved the world that he gave his only son so that you might live?" She pointed at me, momentarily forgetting her scars, the sleeves flouncing above her wrists, scaly purple flesh revealed. I stared, wondering what had happened to her.

"Tell me how you met Isabel."

"At church," I said, "but before that, I saw her in the woods behind my house. There's a creek there."

"What did you notice about her?"

"She was wearing a bathing suit, playing in the water. Her hair was in a braid."

"But you met her at church?"

I nodded. "I met her at church, but I first saw her in the woods."

"Why didn't you introduce yourself when you saw her in the woods?"

"I don't know. I hid."

"Why did you hide?"

"I don't know."

"But you do know. Tell me."

I rubbed my eyes. I was tired. "I didn't know her," I said. "I didn't know anything about her."

"What happened the next time you saw her?"

Mrs. Dupree had her arms at her sides behind the big desk. She leaned back in her springy chair. "Go on. Tell the story." I'd told it before. I had to tell it again. I had to tell it every day.

"I met her at church, and she invited me to come over to her aunt's house to listen to records."

"What happened next?"

"I don't know. We listened to Beatles records. She taught me to do the mashed potato and some other dances."

"Then what happened?"

I told Mrs. Dupree how things progressed. How we moved from dancing to hand holding to kissing. If I left out a detail, she corrected me. I spoke repeatedly about the beginning, middle, and ending of our relationship. Mrs. Dupree never tired of hearing about the last chapter, the part where we were caught, where Isabel's aunt flipped on the light switch, two police officers standing behind her. Isabel and I were naked, a pink sheet balled up between us.

"What were you two doing before you were caught?"

She wanted details.

"Kissing."

"Kissing where?" Her sleeves flounced up to her elbows and she smoothed them down. "I need remorse, Gloria. Where did you put your mouth? Where did she put her mouth? Why were the police there?"

I replayed the scene every day, sometimes more than once in a session. My mouth had been in a private place, a place where it didn't belong. The police were there because my parents had been in a car accident. They'd come to take me to the hospital. Mrs. Black, Isabel's aunt, had thrown my clothes at me. I'd been mortified, terrified, even as the police said, "Your parents are going to be okay, just cuts and bruises."

"You sinned," Mrs. Dupree said, "but it doesn't matter how many times I say it. You're the one who has to say it. You have to own it. You have to confess what you did. You have to confess that it was wrong and ask the Heavenly Father to forgive and guide you."

"I was wrong." I remembered Isabel there, standing on her aunt's porch in a pink silk robe, biting her painted nails, her dark hair fallen down about her face. "It'll be okay," I told her. "I'll see you tomorrow." Then I ducked into the back of the police car, but it wasn't okay. It would never be okay after that.

At the hospital, a nurse took me to see my father first. He'd been driving. He'd swerved to miss a deer. When he saw me, he smiled, holding up his bandaged left hand as explanation. "I can't move my fingers, but I can move my thumb a little bit."

Then, I saw my mother. She looked terrible: bruises for eyes. The lower part of her face was bandaged. I tried to hold her, but I was afraid that I would hurt her. "Oh, Mommy," I said, "are you okay?"

She managed to say, "It hurts to talk." She had gotten twenty-three stitches at the jawline. My mother said, "I'll have a scar."

Mrs. Dupree said, "What happened next?"

"I telephoned Isabel's house. Her aunt picked up and said, 'Don't you think you've done enough? You're a terrible girl.'"

"And then? Did you know that she was telling the truth? That you had done a terrible thing?"

"Isabel left a note on my front porch. It said that she was leaving, that I would never see her again."

Mrs. Dupree shook her head. "What did you think?"

"I thought that she couldn't mean it. I thought that she loved me."

"But she didn't, did she? She used you."

I remembered my mother wore lipstick. She looked like a clown with the black eyes and red lips, the stitches like a horror show. She and my father came home. "Mrs. Black telephoned my parents. She told them what she knew."

"And did she say that you'd done a bad thing?"

"I don't know. I guess."

"But you should know, Gloria."

"Isabel went home."

"Why are you here, Gloria, if not to be changed?"

"I don't know anymore."

I was at Belmont because our neighbor Maria Montefusco had a cousin who'd reportedly been cured of homosexuality at the institute. Mrs. Montefusco told my mother, "I bet they can help Gloria. You should give them a call." My parents telephoned the institute and received a discreet brown-paper package, which included a twenty-four-page brochure about the causes and cures for homosexuality. The pamphlet described their nondenominational Christian approach to treating the disease, including detailed information about the four phases that ensured full recovery. Phase one: Removal. It began with the patient's isolation from triggers. No social contact with the outside world. Phase two: Revelation. The patient was guided to reveal his or her sin(s) with as much detail as possible, not once but daily, while the counselor confronted the sinful acts, retelling each perverted story. Then came Admonition, accepting that the acts were wholly deviant. This was the stage with which I was having difficulty. Nothing about my relationship with Isabel had felt deviant or unnatural. Lastly, there was stage four: Forgiveness and Rebirth. All would be forgiven. I would be reborn, released upon the world with a step-by-step plan of action. I would live a happy, normal life in God's light.

Even as my parents read aloud from the booklet, asking if this was something I was willing to try, I wasn't fully listening. "Gloria," my mother said, "we only want to help. You're not eating. You're not talking. We're worried about you. Tell us what you need." In truth, I thought that nothing could be worse than the sadness I felt at losing Isabel. I was dramatic and emotional. I was sixteen, and I was mistaken. The institute was far worse than a broken heart.

6

DAYS PASSED SLOWLY AT THE institute. I was permitted no telephone calls or correspondence because I hadn't repented. Mrs. Dupree and Dr. Belmont needed me to believe that I was sick, that my feelings for Isabel and even Amelia had been part of a greater illness, a sinfulness that was corrupting the very core of my identity. They wanted tears, lots of them. I remembered Sheff telling me to save the boohooing for the counselors. He hadn't exaggerated.

Mrs. Dupree asked about my relationship with my parents, and I told her about the twins, about my mother's depression. "I need details," she said. "Tell me exactly what you remember about the day you lost your mother."

No one had ever put it in those words, but that was precisely how it had felt: not like the day my mother lost the twins, but like the day I lost my mother. I said, "My mother's babies were born too soon."

"You're not listening, Gloria," Mrs. Dupree said. "I need you to really remember. How old were you?"

"Seven?"

"What time was it?"

"I don't know. Early in the morning. When I woke up, she was gone."

"Who was there? Was your father there?"

I shook my head.

"Who was there? Tell me what happened. Start at the beginning. Let yourself go back there. You're safe here. Try to remember."

I didn't want to remember.

"Tell me the story," Mrs. Dupree urged. "Tell me your story."

I looked at her before I spoke. Her scars were hidden, her hands clasped together.

I remembered the bees gathered outside my window seat. I'd been watching them since I'd woken up. "It was June second. The babies weren't supposed to come until August."

"Good," she said. "Keep going. You're at your house. What do you see, Gloria?"

"Grace Kelly."

"Excuse me?"

"On the cover of *Life* magazine."

"What else?"

"Bees."

"Where are the bees?"

"They're swarming where I threw up."

"When did you throw up? Never mind. Let's start at the beginning. See it in your mind's eye. God is in there with you. You believe in the Holy Spirit, don't you?"

I did. "I do."

"Then, relax. Start at the beginning. Start when the sun came out." She talked with her hands. Her sleeves flounced up to her forearms. Her burn scars were exposed to the natural light coming through the window. She was so caught up with my story, she forgot to hide them.

I remembered Gwen Babineaux standing at the kitchen counter, drinking a cup of coffee. "My neighbor was there. She asked me what I wanted for breakfast. I asked her, 'Where's my mom?' and she said, 'Your mom had to go to the hospital, and your dad went too.'

"I asked Mrs. Babineaux, 'Is she okay?' and she said, 'I'm sure everything will be fine. Your dad's going to call as soon as he knows something.' Then, she made scrambled eggs and toast and told me I had to eat, but I wasn't hungry. I was worried about my mother."

"You're doing great, Gloria," Mrs. Dupree said.

"I remember that Mrs. Babineaux said, 'You should pray for your mother.' Then the telephone rang, and I tried to get it. I thought it would be my father, telling me that my mother and the babies were coming home from the hospital.

Mrs. Babineaux reached over and grabbed the receiver before I could get it. I went and sat at the kitchen table. That's where Grace Kelly was. There was a full-color photograph of her and Prince Rainier III of Monaco on the magazine cover. I was looking at that photograph when Mrs. Babineaux said, 'Oh no.'

"Then I was looking at her. 'What's happening?' I asked. 'Is Mother okay?'

"She shook her head. 'Oh no. I'm so sorry.'

"Then I ran through the den, out the front door to the stoop, where the honeybees zipped from tulip to tulip. The sun was shining. I threw up the scrambled eggs and toast I'd eaten. Then, one of the bees landed on my scalp and stung me. It felt like an electric charge. My skin, every pore, pulsing. Someone once told me that the skin is the body's largest organ, and I remember that when I got stung, my whole body shuddered, the poison seemed to surge from nerve to nerve, connect-the-dots, a million needles piercing me. I had never felt so alive and so simultaneously vulnerable. Even as Mrs. Babineaux came onto the porch, resting her hand on my back, I was feeling that sting: Was my mother going to be okay?

"Mrs. Babineaux sat beside me, gathering her robe between her legs. 'Your mother's going to be just fine,' she said.

"I was so relieved, I bent forward and sobbed. Then Mrs. Babineaux said, 'The boys didn't make it.'

"I didn't understand what she meant.

"'They were just too small. Your baby brothers are with God now.' She kept talking, but I stopped listening, feeling that sting, a honeybee flitting in and out of my peripheral vision."

Mrs. Dupree said, "How was your mother when she came home?"

"She wasn't fine. She was sad."

Mrs. Dupree shook her head. Then, she saw her burns and smoothed down her sleeves. "I'm sorry, Gloria, for you and for your mother. This is really an important breakthrough. I think it's possible that your attraction to females stems from your mother's desertion." She made notes on her pad of paper.

"She didn't desert me." Even as I said this, I remembered the woman my mother had been before the twins died. She was funny. I had memories of her puffing on my father's cigar, doing impressions of Groucho Marx, baking bread and chocolate-chip cookies, sitting in the backyard reading dog-eared paperbacks, reciting her favorite parts. Our bookshelves were lined with famous American authors like Cheever, O'Connor, Welty, Hemingway, and Faulkner, and poets like Langston Hughes, Robert Lowell, and Elizabeth Bishop. She was always reading and rereading her favorite books. "Good prose is poetry and vice versa," she would tell me. I remembered her reading Bishop aloud. The cover looked like a mainsail and jib. There was this one poem, "The Fish," my favorite, and this one line about how the "oil spread a rainbow around the rusted engine," how "everything was rainbow, rainbow, rainbow." I remembered the way she said it with such force, such passion. She could recite the whole thing. The words really meant something to her.

Before the twins came, I had asked her if she'd always wanted to be a housewife, and she'd laughed. "Not exactly. It's what you do, Gloria . . ." Then, she'd smiled. "But I knew this boy before your father." I remember that we were in the kitchen, rolls rising on the counter, the smell of yeast permeating the room. She had this otherworldly, sweet look on her face. "It was so long ago. I guess he was my first boyfriend. He went to Columbia. He wanted me to be unconventional." I was five or six. I didn't know what *unconventional* meant. She explained, "He wanted me to break the rules. We used to meet on the roof of our building and talk about literature and philosophy." She laughed. "He always called me Red, never Molly."

"Before you met Dad?" I asked.

"Of course before your father." She smiled again. "A long time ago."

"Were you in love with him?"

"No."

"What happened to him?"

"He moved. That's all."

"Did he want you to move with him?"

"Yes, but you didn't do that. That's not what you did. That's not what I did." Whenever she felt nostalgic, she talked about philosophers, poetry, and the boy who went to Columbia.

After the twins died, she was a different person. She rarely talked about the boy, gave up the Groucho Marx impersonations and the cookie baking. She stacked her favorite books like a pagoda on the coffee table. She was going to donate them to a church sale. Mrs. Babineaux was flipping through one when my mother said, "Take them, Gwen. Take whatever you want."

"I'll borrow them," Mrs. Babineaux said. "You might want them back."

"They're all yours."

I remembered trailing Mrs. Babineaux to the door. I wanted the Bishop. I needed the poem about the fish. I needed those rainbows. At the front door, Mrs. Babineaux patted my arm. "Things will get back to normal soon."

But I knew they wouldn't. It felt like we were past the point of no return. "I want the Bishop," I said.

"Which one is that?"

I pulled it from her pile.

Mrs. Babineaux bent down and kissed my cheek.

For the rest of that awful year, the bees trailed me. When my bedroom window was closed, they butted against it. I thought they were a sign, a reminder that my life was not going to be like Grace Kelly's.

Mrs. Dupree and I made a breakthrough. My mother was to blame. It was hard to fathom. Mrs. Dupree said, "Tell me about life after the twins died. What changed?"

Everything had changed, but I knew she wanted specifics, so I told her about the Lavach family, how I was sent each morning to their house when my father went to work. Gwen Babineaux and her husband, Eugene, were on holiday in Switzerland. Otherwise, I would've gone there.

I said, "Mr. and Mrs. Lavach had four daughters: Peggy, sixteen; Whitney, fourteen; Lucy, eleven; and Sparky, eight. Sparky's given name was Connie, short for Constance, but everyone called her Sparky because when she was four, she stuck a bobby pin in a light socket. Sparky was a year older than me. I didn't really like her or her sisters, and I don't think they liked me, but I had no choice in the matter. When I asked my father why I couldn't stay home, he said, 'Because your mother doesn't feel well.'

"It felt like the longest summer of my life. Every day, we piled into Mrs. Lavach's station wagon, and she took us to the community pool. The older girls made fun of my swimsuit, how it sagged down one thigh. Sparky held me underwater, and whenever I tried to be alone, to sit under the umbrella with a notebook and write, Mrs. Lavach said, 'Go play with the others.' She drank Bloody Marys. I remember that there was a red lipstick print on the rim of the glass, her celery stalk sticking out."

Mrs. Dupree said, "Tell me about your notebooks. You brought two here with you."

"And I'd like them back please."

"Tell me about them." She leaned forward, and once again, I could see her scars. Again, I wondered what had happened to her.

"I was keeping a diary at first," I said, "and I'd write about my mother, how long she'd been sad, when the twins had died, what I expected them to be like if they'd lived. I named them William and Erik."

44

"Keep going."

"But then I started writing stories. I wrote about a woman, a Joan of Arc figure in chain mail, armed with a steel sword. She swept across the nation of Lana in pursuit of a wicked queen. In my story, the queen had once been good and just, but then someone stole her soul and locked it in a box. Joan planned to find the box and release the queen's soul, but in the meantime, she had to fight the queen and her army. Joan didn't want to hurt or kill the queen. She wanted to save her."

"Did the queen have a name?"

"No. Just 'queen.'"

"And the warrior was called Joan?"

"Yes, like Joan of Arc. She had short hair and pretended to be a boy." I knew that I was the warrior, but I wasn't going to offer that insight to Mrs. Dupree. She could figure it out on her own. I continued, "The story ended with a huge battle. Joan wounded the queen. The queen was going to die, but then Joan had a vision. The box that held the queen's soul was under a mossy log. Before the queen died, Joan found the box and opened it. The soul escaped, returning to the queen, and she woke up as if from a nightmare. She was her old kind and good self. She smiled and laughed and ate her daughter's mud pies. Basically, I wrote the happy ending that I wanted. I wanted animal-shaped pancakes. Instead, I got a bowl of soggy corn flakes and a mother who slept most of the day. I remember begging her to tell me stories about the college boy. Recite the fish poem for me. Do something, anything that resembled my mother. By the time I was eight, I knew the fish poem by heart."

Mrs. Dupree adjusted her sleeves again and wrote more notes. I waited, hoping we were done for the day. She kept writing, and then she looked up. "Who's been raising you? Who took care of you?"

I shook my head, then tucked my hands under my thighs. "I don't know."

"Think."

"The sisters at St. Catherine's. Our neighbor Gwen Babineaux."

Mrs. Dupree stood up from her desk. Beyond her, through the eight-paned window, I could see the sun illuminating the pin oaks and green lawn. "You've made real progress today, Gloria. I feel like we're getting somewhere." She came over to my side of the desk. The timer dinged, and she picked it up. "Tomorrow, you'll read the note from Isabel."

"Wait," I said. "It's me."

"What's you?"

I had my own breakthrough. "I've been taking care of myself."

7

Dear Gloria,

I hope and pray that your parents are all right.

    I'm going home to Batesville, leaving tomorrow. I'm
sorry that things ended so awkwardly. All summer, you
talked about our future together, and all summer, I told you
that I was going home. We don't have a future. I've tried to
be honest with you. After I graduate, I'm marrying Darwin
Weeks, and he can't find out about us. You and I had a lot
of fun, but then we got caught. I'm sorry.

Your friend,
Isabel

From them on, we began therapy with the letter. Every day, I read it aloud, and every day, Mrs. Dupree asked, "Do you think she loved you?"

"I guess not."

"Do you think she loved you, Gloria? Come on."

"It doesn't sound like it."

"Do you think she loved you?"

"No!"

Over and over, the same thing. I lost my sense of time, not day to day, but week to week and month to month. I could distinguish Saturday from Monday because of my daily routine, and I always looked forward to Friday socials, to dancing with Sheff, but ninety minutes, five days a week, I sat across from Mrs. Dupree, repeating the same stories, reading the same letter. I was exhausted, my brain fried.

"Do you feel sexually attracted to your mother?"

"No! God, no!"

"Are you certain?"

"Yes! Of course."

"I don't understand," she said. "Are you sexually attracted to your mother?"

"No, I'm not."

"But you're not certain."

"I am certain." I started crying, not because of guilt, acceptance, revelation, admonition, not for any of their reasons, but because I was beat down, because everything in my life before Belmont started to sound made-up, unreal, like I was losing myself. I wanted my own bed, my front yard, my books, my father, my neighbor, even my sad mother, all the things I'd taken for granted. Freedom.

In December, I received a care package: chocolate bars, chewing gum, and two issues of *Photoplay*. It was the "Guys, Girls, and Guns" issue. Sean Connery was on the cover promoting his new film, *Thunderball*. I read the magazine cover to cover, and slipped it under my pillow. The second issue featured Elizabeth Taylor and Richard Burton. I savored each word.

Every Friday, I clung to Sheff as we danced across the ballroom floor. "Don't let them get to you," he said.

"I'm trying." I held fast to his shirt collar, occasionally glancing down at the glossy tiles, the little squares that made up the country scene. I understood how an outsider would perceive Belmont as a fine, respectable place, and who would tell them otherwise? Parents weren't permitted within the institution except on guided tours where they were shown what they wanted to see: well-dressed, seemingly well-adjusted youths.

It was mid-December. I had hoped to be home for Christmas, but it didn't seem like that was going to happen. I worried that Sheff would be released before me, and he had the same worries. Neither of us wanted to be left behind. "Maybe we'll get out on the same day," I told him.

"Wouldn't that be something."

"I bet stranger things have happened."

"Undoubtedly." He smiled.

I pressed my chin to his collarbone.

He said, "If I went with girls, I'd be with you forever."

"Same here, except with guys, I mean."

The more Belmont tore me down, dismantling everything I knew about myself, the more determined I was to hold on to the young girl who'd loved Amelia, to the young woman who'd loved Isabel. Maybe I was a sexual pervert by Belmont's standards, but my feelings had been legitimate, and I recognized very clearly that Mrs. Dupree was trying to turn me into someone I wasn't. I told Sheff, "I would rather hang myself than spend another ninety minutes with that woman, except that they won't let me have anything with which to hang myself."

He half laughed, but then his voice turned serious. "It gets to you. I know. It gets to me, but the good news is that you got a package. They don't give just anybody packages and letters. It's a sign that they think you're making real progress."

From the turntable speakers, Frank Sinatra crooned "Fly Me to the Moon." Sheff spun me, then pulled me in close. "You'll get out soon. I know it. Me . . . I'm never getting the fuck out of here."

"Yes, you are," I said. "They can't keep you here forever."

"Pop has a lot of money. He can keep me here until I'm eighteen."

"He wouldn't do that."

"Oh, wouldn't he? He fucking hates me."

We were both quiet. It was a gray December, outside and inside Belmont. Sheff said, "I have good news."

"What is it?"

"David went home."

"Which one's he?"

"He had the short pants, like knickers."

"Oh yeah. He seemed nice."

"He did that aversion therapy."

"How did it go?"

"I don't know. No one saw him."

"Anything that comes with a guarantee sounds like the equivalent of a lobotomy."

"You made a rhyme." Sheff took hold of some of my hair. It had grown a lot since I'd arrived at Belmont. "When I get out of here," he said, "I'm disappearing, going to the city to find my Sal Mineo, and I'm never coming back. All we have to do is hang in there."

"We can do it."

"Of course we can. Look around. Look at this motley crew, a bunch of gender-confused misfits. We should riot or something."

"Riot," I repeated. He slipped his hand up the back of my neck, under my curls.

"Smash windows." His breath was warm and smelled of fruit punch.

"Smash windows," I repeated.

"I'm tougher than I look, Gloria."

"Oh, you don't have to tell me. I'm tough too."

"And I need to get my dick sucked."

"Oh, you had to go and ruin it, didn't you?"

His eyes teared up. "I'm good at ruining things."

"Stop. I'm teasing." The song ended. We walked hand in hand toward the chairs. I was looking at the floor tiles, a carriage, a pink satin shoe, a horse hoof, when he said, "I'm confident of one thing."

"And what's that?"

"We're the best-looking people in here. We should get married just to have the most beautiful children in the world."

"We absolutely should."

Sheff squeezed my hand. "I love you, Gloria Ricci."

"I love you too." When I grew up, I'd marry Sheffield Schoeffler, and I wouldn't even care if he went around getting his dick sucked.

He said, "Don't cry too much. You don't want frown wrinkles. My mother has them, and they're horrendous. She goes to a fancy spa and gets her face burned to get rid of them." He contorted his face.

"You're ridiculous."

"You know what we'll do . . ." He let go of my hand and made a fist, shooting his long white arm toward the ceiling, toward the shimmering light that seemed to fall like snow through his watery blue eyes. "We'll live! We'll live wilder than Dr. Belmont and Mrs. Dupree can fathom. I'll write to you, and you'll meet me in Chelsea. We'll go to all the clubs that Jack Kerouac and Allen Ginsberg go to. We'll sleep in the same room where Dylan Thomas slept. We'll burn like fabulous yellow Roman candles." Then, he whispered, "And I'll fuck Sal Mineo."

Sheff was full of hope. He leaned in and kissed me right smack on the lips. Pulling back, he said, "I have to be amorous of girls if I'm ever going to shake this place from my heels."

I was his girl. He was my guy.

He said, "It's no good being alive if you don't get to live."

I couldn't have agreed more.

8

On Christmas Eve, I was called to Mrs. Winningham's desk. She said, "Your father's on the telephone."

I took the black receiver in hand. "Dad?" I wanted him to hear the desperation in my voice. "Can I come home now?"

"Are they feeding you?"

"I'm ready to come home."

"How are you feeling?"

"I'm much better." I pulled the black cord tight around my pointer finger.

"How's the food?"

"I'm ready to come home."

"Dr. Belmont said that you made a friend. Is he nice?"

"He's great. Can I come home?"

"Are you eating?"

"Yes, I'm eating."

"We miss you."

"I want to come home. I don't want to be here anymore. Why haven't you written? Why haven't you been to visit?"

"We've tried, Glo, but the doctor said it was detrimental to your progress, and you'd end up staying longer, and we signed a contract when you were admitted." He sighed. "We shouldn't have signed that contract."

"I want to come home." I paused. "Please come get me. Please. I can't stay here any longer. Please help me."

Mrs. Winningham tapped her wristwatch to indicate that my time was up. Then, she said, "You're being terribly dramatic, Miss Ricci."

"Dad, they're making me get off the phone. Someone said that tomorrow is Christmas. Can't you come see me for Christmas? I'm going to miss midnight Mass. Please let me come home. Please come get me." I started to bawl.

"Oh, honey." His voice broke. "We love you."

Mrs. Winningham wrangled the phone from my grasp before I got to say, "I love you too," but I yelled it as Mrs. Winningham spoke into the receiver, "Dr. Belmont will return your call within the hour, Mr. Ricci."

For the next two weeks, I told Mrs. Dupree everything she wanted to hear: I wanted to grow up and get married—be like everybody else; I was a reformed sinner, a reformed instrument of Satan. I could've won an Oscar. We collaborated, writing a plan of action for my eventual release. I would participate in extracurricular activities at St. Catherine's. Specifically, I would join the pep squad. I would attend school dances and sporting events, spend time with my peers. If and when an impure thought came to me, I would pray. I would confess, but most important, if the thoughts persisted, I would contact the institute.

"Do you want to be successful?" Mrs. Dupree asked.

"Of course." I was committed to my betterment. I even agreed to write a testimonial for the institute about their program's effectiveness. Then on January 5, 1966, four-plus months after walking through Belmont's doors, Miss Rondell came to my room and said, "Pack your things. You're going home." I had little to pack. I hurried, standing at attention, tapping my foot. I couldn't believe it. Finally. Miss Rondell escorted me upstairs to Mrs. Dupree's office, where she stood with her back to me, a gentle rain falling outside the eight-paned window. "Your parents are on their way," she said.

"I need to say good-bye to Sheff."

"I'll tell him that you said good-bye."

"We promised to say good-bye if either of us was getting out."

"I didn't make any such promise." She turned to face me. "Did I?"

"No, ma'am." Then, I saw my copy of *The Catcher in the*

Rye, my notebooks, and my letter from Isabel stacked on the chair where I'd sat ninety minutes a day, five days a week, for one hundred twenty days.

"You can take your things. Or you can leave them."

I approached the window. Only after I saw my parents' car coming up the drive did I say, "I'll take them." I unzipped my suitcase, stowing them inside.

Mrs. Dupree watched. "Don't forget what you've learned."

I didn't respond. I could think of nothing but getting out of Belmont. I hated Mrs. Dupree: her voice, her hands, her burns, her timer. I hated her for making me say things I didn't believe.

"It's time," she said, and this time, I was the one in the lead, down the stairs, first in the elevator, first through the door. Outside, the rain blew in sheets, drumming the awning. It'd been fall when I'd arrived, and now it was the middle of winter. Dr. Belmont was already outside talking to my parents. As soon as I crossed the threshold, my mother ran to me, her arms extended, her tears warm on my neck. "I missed you so much," she said, and any resentment that I'd felt toward her washed away beneath the awning of the Belmont Institute. After what I'd experienced, I could hold no grudge against the sadness she'd felt. If nothing else, I was more empathetic to my mother's pain.

My father took hold of my suitcase and hugged me.

Mother said, "Your father was so upset after he talked to you on Christmas Eve. We wanted to come get you right then, but Dr. Belmont said that you were making great progress." Her voice dropped. "And there was the contract." In spite of myself, tears rolled down my cheeks.

"I just want to go home." I pulled the car door open and slipped inside. My father put my suitcase in the trunk. I watched Dr. Belmont in his silver spectacles shake my father's good hand.

Inside the car, my mother said, "Sister Bernadette is excited that you'll be returning to St. Catherine's for the spring."

"I'm looking forward to going back to school." I held my breath. *Let's go already.*

Mrs. Dupree and Dr. Belmont waved good-bye. I looked down at my lap. As soon as we passed through the wrought iron gates, exhaustion took over. I dreamed that Dr. Belmont and Mrs. Dupree sat side by side, their knees touching, in my window seat. They'd never let me go. I woke as we pulled into the driveway. The rain had been replaced by a white fog.

Walking toward the house, Father was talking about someone I didn't know, some man from the phone company. My father had returned to work, part-time for now. He'd regained partial use of his left pointer finger. I smiled. I was genuinely glad to be home, but I couldn't help thinking of Sheff. While I had my freedom, he would be enduring afternoon prayers.

At six o'clock, we had Swanson TV dinners and watched the evening news with Walter Cronkite. During the first commercial, Father said, "I need to tell you again, Gloria, that I'm sorry I didn't come get you."

My mother concurred. "We promised to follow Dr. Belmont's recommendations."

I wasn't mad at them. I was simply determined to live my life on my own terms. As soon as I heard from Sheff, I'd meet him in Chelsea. I'd wasted enough time.

9

I joined the pep squad. We wore blue shorts and white blouses with little blue ties. I had two pompoms, blue and white, and cheered "Rah rah rah," at the girls' basketball games. There was even a picture of me in the 1966 yearbook. Since I'd been home, I'd been making good grades and going to confession. The sisters thought that secretarial school might be a good avenue for me. I could learn to take dictation and work for a doctor or lawyer until I met a nice young man and settled down.

I'd been home a little over a month when I entered my room to find my mother sitting on my bed, the Bishop book in her hands. She held it up as I set my book bag down. "You still have this." She patted the bed for me to come sit. "Do you remember when I used to read from it?"

I showed her how I'd dog-eared the page with the fish poem.

"That's one of my favorites," she said.

"I know. Me too." I started to recite it. She put her arm around me and joined in. "'I caught a tremendous fish and held him beside the boat half out of water, with my hook fast in a corner of his mouth. He didn't fight. He hadn't fought at all.'" We looked at each other and smiled, our voices like music. "'Here and there his brown skin hung in strips like ancient wallpaper, and its pattern of darker brown was like wallpaper . . .'"

After we'd recited the whole poem, she said, "How do you know it?"

"I started memorizing it when I was seven."

"You're kidding."

"I'm not."

"I've been a terrible mother."

"I'm sure there are worse."

She took a deep breath. "I'm going to do better." She patted my knee. "I'm glad you kept the Bishop."

That evening, I helped with dinner. My mother asked if I wanted to go to the movies after Mass on Sunday.

"Sure."

With that oily rainbow between us, my mother took it upon herself to slowly strip away her own ancient wallpaper, finding a middle-aged woman eager to live. While I waited to hear from Sheff, my mother and I started getting to know each other again.

In early April, we went to Moores Pond. We trekked down one of the trails, the sunlight trickling through the oaks and pines. She said, "Do you still have feelings for Isabel Sullivan?"

We never discussed Isabel. "No. No feelings." Then, I paused. "Maybe anger. I thought she was in love with me. She wasn't."

My mother kicked a rock on the path. "A long time ago, when I knew that college boy, the one who went to Columbia, I knew a couple of girls who were that way, the way you were . . ."

"Lesbians?"

She nodded. "They were nice girls."

"Even though they were gay?"

"Of course."

"I might still be that way." I held my breath.

She took hold of my hand. "We shouldn't have sent you to that place, Gloria. I just thought that if they could make you like everybody else, you'd be happier."

As we emerged from the woods, the sunlight glinted on the pond. I let go of her hand and rubbed my eyes.

"Everybody who's that way has a hard time," she said.

I swallowed hard. "I am that way."

"I love you whatever way you are. When I knew the college boy, we went to this bar where everyone was that way."

"You?!" I couldn't believe it.

"I know." She sort of laughed and scratched her nose. "He was a wild one."

"Sounds like it."

"I guess that what I'm trying to say is that all your father and I want is for you to be happy."

I finished out the school year waiting to hear from Sheff. The summer came fast, and with it came my mother's annual Fourth of July party, a tradition she had kept even after the twins died. That first awful year, everyone had whispered that she seemed really good, but my father and I knew the truth. Like so many people, she was good at pretending things were all right when they weren't.

When my mother was growing up, Independence Day had been her favorite holiday. It reminded her of the years she'd spent at her grandparents' estate in Connecticut. There had been rolling hills, a weeping willow to climb, and horse stables just east of the mansion where she took riding lessons. Her grandfather owned an Alfa Romeo and a Cadillac, and she told me how the chrome bumpers and wheels shone in the sunlight. There were parties. The ladies' dresses were silk and sequined and shimmered beneath the stars, and she told me that she would watch from one of the willow's branches as they danced.

By 1939, the house, automobiles, and land had been repossessed. My mother was ten. She and her two sisters, her parents, and her grandparents moved into a two-bedroom tenement on the Lower East Side. She worked part-time at a dry cleaner's, took care of her aging grandparents, and attended school. By the war's end in 1945, she was sixteen, sick of asphalt and walk-ups, desperate for weeping willows and green lawns, some semblance of the American dream she'd glimpsed. But then she met the college boy, and he filled her head with subversive notions. "Run away with me," he told her. "We'll go west. We'll live like gypsies." This was the opposite of her dream. Her heart was set on a manicured lawn and shiny new appliances, the things she saw in magazines, the things she felt she deserved. If only the college boy would finish school and settle down. Get a job. Buy a house. Then she could be with him. But he didn't. Rather, he went west without her.

When she moved to the suburbs with my father, she got some of that American dream back. She got the green lawn, an automobile, a flowering dogwood, and her own bed. (Growing up, she'd slept on a pullout sofa with her middle sister.)

It was in celebration of those magnificent parties from her childhood that she threw her own. It was the one night of the year when she really dressed up. She always wore a tight-fitting red dress with a plunging neckline, her freckled cleavage exposed. She wore her hair teased up in a bouffant. She could've popped out of one of her grandparents' parties. She served finger sandwiches and pâté in addition to the more traditional hamburgers and hot dogs.

The morning of this year's party, the phone rang early. I heard my father whisper, "Not today. This isn't a good time."

"Who was that?"

"Nobody."

I sat at the bar, eating my cereal, while my father scanned the counter. He perused jars of pickles, olives, and sandwich spreads before opening a pickle jar and shoving a whole one in his mouth. *Crunch . . .*

My mother opened the sliding glass door. "Frank, I could use some help with the folding chairs."

"Be right there," he managed as he crunched his pickle. I heard the door slide closed. My father crunched and crunched, pickle juice dripping down his chin.

"Is everything okay?" I asked.

He wiped his chin with the back of his hand. "It's your uncle Eddie. He might be coming here tonight. Don't say anything to your mother."

"How come?" I knew very little about my uncle. Occasionally, he called our house at some ungodly hour and my father would pick up in the bedroom and then take the call in the kitchen. My mother described him as shiftless. He lived in Oxnard, California, with his wife, Eleanor, and his son, Scotty, who was apparently around my age, but I'd never met any of them.

That evening, Father was manning the grill while I delivered sundry highballs to our neighbors and helped Mother with the food. Our yard was framed with tiki torches. Red, white, and blue lights were strung crisscross overhead. There were aluminum chairs farther out on the lawn where partygoers lounged, smoking cigarettes, enjoying their drinks.

I carried a Waldorf salad to my mother. "Put it on the table, darling," she said, adding, "Oh, and could you grab a spoon?"

When I went back inside, there was a man I didn't recognize. His clothing was disheveled, his hair and eyes dark, his face sweaty. He walked purposefully toward the back patio. Instead of sliding the screen door open, he walked into it, his right leg tearing straight through.

"Oh, shit," he said, trying to right the door on its track, his leg caught in the frame. Disentangling himself, he hurled the door to the patio, where it caught a wrought iron chair, toppling it. "Motherfucker!"

The party took a collective gasp. My father stepped forward. "Everybody," he said, "this is my big brother, Eddie."

Picking up the screen door, Eddie carried it between our stunned partygoers, across the patio and summer lawn to the pines, where he chucked it under a canopy of trees. He walked back toward the party, wiping his hands down the front of his shirt. "That's a real piece of crap, Frank. I would've bought something better made. Not that crap." Mother, flushed and sweating, her mouth partway open, stood at Father's side. Uncle Eddie made a finger-gun, pointing it at her. "You look good, Red!"

Red! The college boy had called her Red. She looked like a deer in headlights.

He pulled a pack of Lucky Strikes from his shirt pocket. "What's a guy gotta do to get a drink around here? I thought this was a party!"

My mother said, "I'll make you a drink, Eddie." She turned back toward the house.

"Thanks. I'll have scotch. No ice."

My father said, "He'll have coffee."

My uncle's hair was blue-black by tiki light. My father took him by the arm. "You had to show up drunk?" He guided him into the kitchen. I followed.

Eddie sidled up to my mother. "It's so good to see you."

"We haven't seen you in a long time." Her voice broke.

"Seventeen years," my father added. "You haven't met Gloria."

Uncle Eddie set his drink on the counter before looking me up and down. Then, he embraced me like we were long-lost friends. There was desperation in the way he held me, in the way he didn't let go. I was still in shock that this was my mother's college boy. Did my father know?

Mother said, "That's enough, Eddie."

He said, "Scotty's sixteen. You're about sixteen, aren't you?"

"Seventeen now," I said.

"My wife is screwing a movie mogul." Uncle Eddie wiped his face with his shirt sleeve. "So I decided to head east. The West Coast is overrated. The wife is a bitch." No one in my house said *screwing* or *bitch*, certainly not in public, certainly not in my presence.

Father said, "Language, Eddie."

Mother said, "We should get back to the party, to our guests. It's almost time for the toast." She poured herself another drink.

"Come on, Gloria." I followed her outdoors while mosquitoes, gnats, and all manner of bugs swarmed our kitchen.

Every year, she climbed a red, white, and blue crepe-paper-strewn ladder and made an elaborate toast to her Irish immigrant grandparents. It was tradition to celebrate the grandparents and the American dream, but this year the toast was shorter, and she seemed forlorn, closing with, "My grandparents lost their American dream." Stepping down off the ladder, only Eddie was clapping. Then my father and the others hesitantly joined him.

Maria Montefusco noted, "The toast was a little different this year."

My mother said, "Thanks a lot," and went for another drink.

In the cul-de-sac, my father lit bottle rockets. They popped and burst, stars raining down over our house. My mother went up to him. My uncle trailed. "I want to light one, Frank," she said.

"It's too dangerous."

"Oh, come on."

"Jesus, Frank. Let her light one," my uncle said.

"Please," my mother added. She pleaded until Father handed her the Zippo and a rocket, at which point she *flick-flicked* the lighter, putting the flame to the twisted thread. It sputtered out. She relit the fuse, and this time it crackled.

"Back up, Molly," Father said. Mother clapped her hands together, but she didn't back up. The rocket exploded, soaring through her bouffant, her hair aflame. I ran toward her, as did Father, but Uncle Eddie clobbered her like a linebacker before either of us could get to her. My uncle the college boy was on top of my mother. Orange and green whirligigs filled the sky. The fire was out.

"It was probably her hair spray that caught," my uncle said. "She's fine. Aren't you fine, Red?" They were on the ground, laughing hysterically. My father kicked his brother's shoe. He kicked it again, and my uncle slowly got to his feet, putting his hand out to help my mother up.

Uncle Eddie didn't even know about the twins. With him, two decades had been erased. There'd been no depression, no car accident, no Belmont. My mother could be the high school girl on the roof again. I felt sorry for my dad. I would never know if he knew. I only knew that my mother had loved his brother before him. My mother had done what she was expected to do. I wondered if she would make that same choice if given a second chance.

10

A WEEK AFTER OUR FOURTH of July party, Uncle Eddie started coming to Sunday dinner. Even though my mother insisted that it was rude to discuss politics at the table, Uncle Eddie talked about the war in Vietnam. He'd fought in Korea. "I never should've walked into that recruiter's office." He drank his scotch and, bleary-eyed, told gruesome stories about his own time in Asia. One minute he was talking about a bomb exploding, and the next, he was talking about his wife, Eleanor, how she wore her hair long down her back, how her boyfriend wore a toupee. "He has one of those in-ground swimming pools. My son, Scotty, smokes pot." Then, back to Vietnam, back to Korea. "Eleanor kicked me out," he said, "and the fucking dog wouldn't even come with me. In Utah, I got robbed by a prostitute named Virtue. Now that's irony."

I couldn't help but laugh.

My father said, "Can we not do this in front of Gloria?"

"Why not? She's practically grown." He continued, "Operation Rolling Thunder is a fucking disaster. We need to stay out of Vietnam."

"But we're having Sunday dinner, Eddie," my mother implored.

"Sunday's no different than any other day of the week."

I liked Uncle Eddie. He made Sundays more entertaining. The rest of the week, we had Walter Cronkite on the evening news, telling us, "And that's the way it is," and it didn't sound good, any of it.

In late July, Eddie came to my room after helping my mother with the dishes. "You doing okay?" he asked. "Your mother told me about your girlfriend and that institution." When had my mother told him these things? I wondered. When had they been alone together? Why had she told him?

"I'm doing all right."

"All the best philosophers were queer," he said. "Nothing wrong with it."

"What about you?" I asked. "How are you doing? You never say. Have you talked to your son?"

He lit a cigarette. "I'm all right, I guess. The kid doesn't want to talk to me."

"How come?"

"His mother hates me. I was a shit dad, I guess. They don't want me, and I can't say that I blame them. I've had some issues with mental stability."

"Oh, that's all."

"Yeah, that's all." He lit a cigarette. "You want one?"

"Sure." Isabel and I had smoked together. I pulled one from his pack, and he lit it with his Zippo. Then, I said matter-of-factly, "You used to date my mother." If he was putting his cards on the table, I'd show mine too.

He flicked his cigarette ash in my windowsill. "Did she tell you that?"

"Does my dad know?"

Uncle Eddie brushed his bangs back from his face. "We were just friends. It was a million years ago."

"Did you go to Columbia?"

"Before I dropped out. Look, Gloria, your mom and dad are good people. Your dad was always a good guy. He took care of our mother after I split town."

"I didn't know that."

"Our father left her and us when I was fifteen and Frank was twelve. Left us for another woman. Got an annulment and made me and Frankie bona fide bastards."

"He never told me."

"It was more than our mother could take, but he was the good guy who didn't run out on people. If you're looking for mental stability, your dad's got it in spades."

I flicked my ash on top of Eddie's. "I like my dad."

"You should."

☙

One week later, I got a letter from Sheff: *I'm having a gay time in New York. Write to me. I'm waiting!* Finally! Had his pop kept him at Belmont this whole time, or had he been busy with his Sal Mineo?

It didn't matter. I wouldn't feel slighted by some Sal Mineo look-alike. I wrote back immediately:

Dear Sheff,

I've really missed you. I need a couple weeks to make arrangements. I have seventy-three dollars saved from birthdays and Christmases. I'll write soon.

Love,
G

I thought that since Uncle Eddie was a rogue adventurer, he'd agree to take me to the train station. I was mistaken: "Are you insane? You'll break your mother's heart, Gloria."

We were sitting on the back patio after Sunday dinner. Hundreds of fireflies blipped on and off. "It's just a ride. No big deal."

"Where are you going? Are you going to see that girl?"

"No. I don't care about her anymore."

"Then, where are you going?"

"I'm seventeen. I'll be eighteen in seven months. I'm going to see a friend who needs me. It's important."

Uncle Eddie slipped off his loafers, resting his bare feet in a chair. "Where does your friend live?"

"I don't want to say."

"No can do."

"Come on. I'm just asking for a ride to the train station. If you won't take me, I'll hitchhike there."

He shook his head. "No."

"I have a friend who lives a block from the train station. Can you give me a ride to her house?"

"Is she a real person?"

"Sure."

He sighed. "You're doing this no matter what, aren't you?"

I nodded.

"Will you promise to write and let your parents know that you're all right?"

"Of course."

"Promise."

"I pinky swear." I thought of Sheff.

"Come on, then." Uncle Eddie and I latched pinkies.

"I'll send a postcard as soon as I get there."

"But I don't know anything about any of this."

"Of course not." I added, "You're a softie."

"I'm something."

A week later, while my dad was at work and my mother was shopping, Uncle Eddie picked me up. On the way to the station, we passed St. Catherine's Parochial School, the marble statue of Our Lady of Perpetual Help, the Maryville Theater, Edith's Bakery, and Gino's Italian Restaurant. As we drove farther on, the boxy houses, narrow streets, and green lawns expanded into industrial sprawl. I had second thoughts but kept them to myself. I was going to see Sheff. We would live how we pleased. That was all that mattered.

When we pulled into the station depot, Uncle Eddie said, "Are you sure about this?"

"I am. I have to go see him."

"Your friend's a him?"

"My friend's a him." I grabbed my suitcase and leaned in through the passenger-side window to say thank you.

"Don't make them worry. Did you leave a note?"

I nodded.

"And what does it say?"

"Don't worry."

"I hope it said more than that."

It did. I'd written:

Dear Mother and Father,

I love you both very much, but there's a friend I need to go

see. I'm nearly eighteen, and I'll finish school in good time.
Don't worry about me. I'll write to you.

Love always,
Gloria

I thanked my uncle, and he shook his head. "Be careful, please."

"I will."

An hour and twenty minutes later, I emerged in Grand Central Station, with its vaulted ceilings, crystal chandeliers, immense columns, and pedestals topped with golden bees. I was breathless. When I was twelve, Mrs. Babineaux had taken me to New York to see Mary Martin play Peter Pan, but we'd taken the transit train to Penn Station. It wasn't golden like Grand Central Station. There'd been no golden bees.

Stepping onto East 42nd, I spotted Sheffield waiting for me. I smoothed my red pants and checked the buttons on my sleeveless blouse. My suitcase was the same red as my outfit. It was the same suitcase I'd taken to Belmont. I figured it deserved a good time.

Sheff wore a mod blazer, the collar upturned, a cigarette dangling from his bottom lip. I slipped between the tourists and commuters, sneaking up behind him, tapping his shoulder. Seeing me, he proclaimed, "We did it! We fucking did it!"

He pulled me in close, then blew a plume of smoke over my head as he released me. "I missed the shit out of you, G." He picked up my suitcase.

I said, "Same here," and ran my hand through his coarse blond locks. Overhead, a jet plane passed through the late-summer sky. The sun was low, blocked by skyscrapers. Sheff's eyes matched the remaining light. It was one of those rare moments in time—the blond-haired boy, the smoky blazer, the crape myrtles and verbena in bloom, the jet plane overhead, the pretzel vendor, a violinist playing for change, everything converging—that felt so tangible, everlasting, that I could hold it in my hand, slip it in my pocket, and pull it out to remember whenever it suited me: whether a week, ten weeks, a year, even ten years later. I could keep it forever.

On the way to the hotel, we stopped in front of the New York Public Library, the library lions just above us. I said, "My mother used to talk about the library lions, about Patience and Fortitude, the qualities the city needed in order to survive the Great Depression. Her grandparents and parents lost everything."

"My pop says that we Schoefflers never lose."

"Speaking of your pop, what happened? I thought he was keeping you at Belmont until you turned eighteen." Sheff pulled a pair of sunglasses from his jacket pocket and pushed them up his nose.

"I don't know," he said. "I just kept telling that fucker Dr. Belmont everything he wanted to hear. I confessed until he believed every word I said."

"Really?" I was incredulous. But it didn't matter why Dr. Belmont had released him. We were here.

"I'm an amazing actor," Sheff continued. "That's why I go for the Sal Mineo types. Maybe I'll have a future in pictures." Then, he trailed me up the library steps. There were people snacking on the steps.

"It's beautiful," I said.

"If I had a camera, I'd take your picture." He put his arm around me. "Let's get a move on, Blondie."

As we walked south down Sixth Avenue, the crowd thinned. Sheff offered me a cigarette, and I took it. "So what happened with Sal Mineo?"

"He split with another guy. Sal looked good, but there was nothing going on upstairs." Sheff swung my suitcase. "I got to see Allen Ginsberg."

"You're kidding me."

"I didn't get to meet him, but I saw him. I could've met him. I even had a copy of *Howl* in my back pocket, but I couldn't speak. No words. Can you imagine me speechless? Of course not. Me either. I was so embarrassed. There were twenty people hanging around the lobby of the hotel, talking to him, and I went mute. I wished you were with me. Between the two of us, we could've summoned the courage."

"Nah. I probably would've gone mute too." He was smiling. He took off his sunglasses to wipe the perspiration from his brow. The collar of his blazer flopped down between his shoulder and jaw. His eyes were bloodshot. "Are you sleeping?"

"Not for shit. The stupid door from the balcony to my room won't shut all the way. I pile stuff against it, but it bangs when it's windy, and the neighbors are noisy. Man, G, I missed you."

"I missed you more."

"So, what's been going on?"

I told him about the pep squad, about how I'd tried to say good-bye to him before I left Belmont, but there'd been no forewarning that I was going home, and they wouldn't let me say good-bye. I started to tell him about my uncle and my mother, but I didn't know where to begin.

"Oh, they never let you say good-bye. You can bet it's in the contract."

I laughed. "That stupid fucking contract."

The Chelsea was not what I expected. Everything was shabby, from the front desk to the sunken sitting area with its mismatched cigarette-burned velveteen sofas to the broken elevator. We hiked our way up to the twelfth floor, down the hall to Sheff's room, the door open. He flung his arms wide. "Check it out."

It wasn't much. A mattress on a metal frame, a rickety bed-side table, a pair of French doors leading onto a tiny balcony, where a dead chrysanthemum lolled back and forth. The balcony's red paint was flaking, revealing patches of shiny, shiny metal. "Posh digs," I said.

"Only the best." Sheff pulled off his boots and dropped to the mattress. I lay beside him. "Check it out." He pointed at the ceiling. "The water stain looks like a fat man. I call him Harry."

"Nice to meet you, Harry."

The doors were open. Humidity and the smell of refuse rose, a musk, up from the asphalt. The dead chrysanthemum's pot clanked the railing. Sheff lit a cigarette and took a swig of vodka, passing the bottle to me. It burned all the way down. I said, "I'm missing a basketball game."

"I didn't know you played."

"I don't. I'm on the pep squad. I pep."

"No offense, but are you really all that peppy?"

I took another swig. "Nope. Not really. Like you, I'm a great actor."

He laughed. "I was on the debate team in junior high. I was pretty good, but I didn't like arguing."

"Then, you weren't pretty good."

He rolled onto his side. "You're right, but I was on the team." He pulled a canvas bag from the bedside table. "Are you hungry?" He had a sleeve of saltines and potted meat. I thought how my father would've liked Sheff. He never went anywhere without saltines. He had the crazy idea that since salt was a preservative, it was good for you. Any doubts that I'd had about coming to New York dissipated. My parents didn't need me, but Sheff certainly did.

11

THAT FIRST WEEK, SHEFF AND I took the D train to Coney Island. Where the subway exited onto the street, there was a clapboard kiosk manned by a tall woman wearing a sequined mermaid tail and halter top. She wore glitter on her cheeks and sat perched on a stool beside a thin, shirtless man in cutoff shorts. He sold postcards of the mermaid.

"I'll sign one for you," she said.

Sheff said, "I've always wanted to meet a real live mermaid."

The mermaid applied bright red lipstick and kissed two postcards for us. "Fifty cents," she said. Well worth it.

We walked down Surf Avenue, past the amusement rides. Shrill laughter and screams tunneled down the boardwalk. Bikini-clad roller skaters whizzed past while jugglers and stilt walkers paraded by. Placards advertised dancing girls and escape artists. A student of

Houdini's was performing upstairs from a magic shop. We stopped to listen to a man playing saxophone, and dropped another fifty cents in his case. In the afternoon, we popped into a pizza joint just down from Nathan's Famous Hot Dogs to get a slice and a Coke. Finishing my slice, I wrote my postcard: *Dear Mother and Father, I am doing well. Safe and sound. I'll write again soon. I promise. P.S. I met a real live mermaid (pictured here)! I love you. Gloria.* I accidentally left a greasy fingerprint on the card. Sheff and I walked to the post office, where I slipped my card in the mail slot.

"What happened when you got home?" he asked.

"My parents said they were sorry."

"Maybe I should've moved in with you."

"They just want me to be happy."

"God, you're lucky. Why'd you ever come to Chelsea?"

"For you. Because we promised."

"Thank you."

Sheff and I walked down Neptune Avenue, back toward the shore. Around 28th Street, we took off our shoes and dodged the surf. Everything felt wide-open. There were no high-rises and no boxy houses in neat rows. Just water and sky as far as the eye could see. We could swim out and go on forever if we chose. Dusk came, and with it, like a mirage, a purple flag and circus-style tent seemed to rise up from the sand.

"Was that there?" I asked.

"I guess so. Come on." Sheff took my hand. Outside the yellow-and-orange-striped tent, the face of a gypsy with big hoop earrings and a crystal ball was painted on a placard. "This will be cool,"

he said. *The One and Only Madame Zelda, Fortune-Teller, Gypsy.*
"Sure. Why not?"

As I stepped under the flap, into the cool darkness, a flurry
of bees swarmed above my head. "What in the world?" They
hovered, and I swatted, before they exited the tent in a straight
line. Madame Zelda sat at a round table, her figure partly shadowed. She had a hook nose and long arthritic fingers adorned
with gold-banded red and yellow stones; her hands splayed
across the table. "Sit. Sit," she said.

We sat on two wooden crates. Madame Zelda said, "The
bees came with you, girl."

Sheff elbowed me. "This is cool."

She pulled a can out from beneath the table, where the purple
velvet drapery flowed down, blending with her own skirt. "One
dollar for the both of you." Sheff pulled a buck from his wallet.

"Where's your crystal ball?" I asked.

"I don't need a ball to see your fortune. Just your hand." Madame Zelda took hold of Sheff's left hand and my right hand,
closing her eyes. Sheff and I smiled at each other. One of us was
going to bust out laughing, I knew it, but then Madame Zelda
seemed to convulse. Her body vibrated, her grip on my hand
tightened, and I felt something like an electrical current shoot
through my arm, into my chest, a sharp pain as her head jerked
back. I tried to pull my hand free, but couldn't. Sheff started
laughing. I felt a terrible pain in my neck and in the back of
my head as Madame Zelda jerked forward, releasing our hands.
Her eyes were white. Empty. "Good trick," Sheff said.

Madame Zelda said, "You're not alone, girl." She closed her eyes, opening them to reveal dull brown irises.

Sheff said, "Tell my fortune."

She said, "You're touched, girl. The spirit world knows you. It's met you and held on."

I stood. "No one knows me."

Madame Zelda said, "When you were a little girl, the bees drank from your sadness. They don't forget. You're a part of them."

"No, I'm not." How could she know about the bee sting, the sadness? She was guessing. She couldn't. Everybody's sad sometimes.

"The bees come from the other side."

"What side?" Sheff grinned. "Now, do me. This is so worth a buck."

I sat.

Madame Zelda regarded Sheff. "Give me your hand again." She cradled it between her own and closed her eyes. Nothing happened. After a minute, she let go and patted his hand. "I'm sorry, boy. I don't see anything." She stood. Her purple skirt swooshed the sandy floor. "With you, girl, I see some kind of trouble. The bees carry the spirits here from the other side. They're watching over you."

Sheff said, "Do you think I'm going to be rich and famous?"

"Whatever you want," she said.

When we got back to the city, the sickle moon hung low between two skyscrapers. I felt unnerved. I didn't like Madame Zelda or what she had to say.

12

IN EARLY SEPTEMBER, WE RENTED a rowboat at Turtle Pond in Central Park. It was a warm day. Sheff's eyes matched the sky's reflection in the pond. The turtles swam and sunned themselves on rocks while dragonflies zipped across our boat. Then, a fish jumped out of the water, and I told Sheff about the fish poem, reciting the first few lines. I said, "I think Mrs. Dupree was right about one thing."

"And what's that?"

"I think I was mad at my mother for a long time, but after Belmont, I feel like I got her back."

"I never had mine," Sheff said.

As he rowed near the shore, hundreds of honeybees swarmed a patch of bamboo. I pointed. "The day that I found out that my mother had lost the twins, I was stung."

"Just like Madame Zelda said." He smiled. "They've come to help you."

"Lucky me."

Sheff rowed past the bees toward the pussy willows on the other side of the pond. We stretched out, floating among the flowering reeds and lily pads, listening to the frogs. When our rental was nearly up, Sheff said, "Let's stay another hour." We rowed over toward the men renting boats to let them know. One of them had an Italian accent. "It is a perfect day for two lovebirds." We grinned and thanked him.

That night, we went to a second-run theater and watched *The Plague of the Zombies*. We sat in the back, laughing at the zombies and noshing popcorn. Sheff said, "I could play a zombie."

"I thought that's what you've been doing." He never slept through the night.

"Ha-ha."

We got back to our room at two a.m. Sheff fell asleep first. Lying close to him, I whispered in his ear, "I'm going to marry you, Sheffield Schoeffler." I said it how Mary said it to George in his bad ear in *It's a Wonderful Life*.

The days passed quickly. Sheff was like a child's spinning top, compelled by cute boys and smoky jazz clubs. He never stopped twirling, preferring life this way, never slowing down, never stopping to think, to consider consequences. I'd been in New York two weeks when I realized that he was turning tricks. Middle-aged men, men my father's age, put five- and ten-dollar bills down on our table at the club, the Big Panda, and Sheff said, "I'll be right back," before disappearing into the bathroom.

When I confronted him, he said, "It's no big deal. It's easy money."

I countered, "But it is a big deal."

"Not to me."

Nearly every night, we went to the Big Panda for the jazz music, for Sheff to turn tricks. "Why don't we get real jobs?" I asked.

"Because this is easy," he said. "These old guys, half of them come before they even have their pants down, G."

"I'll get a job."

"If that's what you want, then go ahead. I don't want a real job."

In mid-September, I started working at Bart's Vinyl three days a week, alphabetizing the stacks of records customers perused and put back in the wrong place. Additionally, I had the horrendous task of cleaning the unisex bathroom, which, like the Big Panda men's room, was used as more than just a toilet. The owner, Bart, paid me under the table: one dollar an hour, fifty cents less than the minimum wage, about thirty dollars a week, a pittance, and Sheff kept turning tricks despite my insistence that I could get a second job, make enough to pay our rent.

Every week, I sent a postcard home, telling my parents not to worry. *I'm safe, getting plenty to eat.* I even considered going home for Christmas; I missed my parents, but I didn't want to leave Sheff. He sometimes disappeared after turning a trick, and I'd find him back at our hotel, high on a mix of alcohol and pills. He liked depressants, things that stopped him from spinning and put him to sleep. It was the in-between he couldn't take.

In mid-December, we went to Central Park to hook up with these college kids I'd met at Bart's Vinyl. I thought the girl, Genevieve, was pretty, and the boy, Paul, said that he thought Sheff was cute. Beforehand, Sheff and I went to Dick's Donuts for cherry Danish and filled our coffees with bourbon. We sat on orange stools and spun ourselves dizzy. It was a good night. Genevieve was freckly and bubbly, and she had good taste in music. Her friend Paul was tall and thin. They were best friends like me and Sheff. They were both art history majors at Columbia—of all places.

I wore tights and a long wool dress I'd gotten at the thrift store. Sheff wore his wool peacoat. When I saw Genevieve, I shouted, "We brought bourbon." Paul shouted back, "We have ginger ale." Sheff and I ran to catch up with them. Genevieve carried a blanket rolled up under her arm. We picnicked beside a willow, and I poured bourbon and ginger into Dixie cups. After a few rounds, Paul asked Sheff if he wanted to take a walk. I was anxious about being alone with Genevieve. I hadn't kissed a girl since Isabel. Even though I knew Dr. Belmont and

Mrs. Dupree were wrong about everything, I'd thought a lot about who I was, about what it meant to like girls, if God was okay with it. I reasoned that if God did so love the world that he offered up his only son, maybe he would love me enough to let me be myself.

Genevieve's freckles were practically black in the darkness. She said, "There's a new exhibit at the MoMA."

"What is it?"

"Mutoscopes. It should be pretty neat."

I stared at her mouth, wondering if I should try to kiss her, wondering if she wanted to kiss me. She said, "Mutoscopes were these machines where one person could watch a sort of early motion picture. A series of cards flipped inside the machine. They have the machines and cards on display. Paul's already been. He said it's worth seeing."

"Neat."

She leaned in and kissed me, then stopped. "Maybe we could go sometime. To see the Mutoscopes."

"Yes."

She kissed me again, one hand on my thigh, sliding up under my sweater dress. Heat spread out from between my thighs. I kept thinking, *I'm not doing anything wrong*, and then I wasn't thinking. I was untethered, slipping my hand inside her jacket, under the hem of her shirt. She felt good. I felt good. Then, I heard Sheff call out, "We're back." Genevieve pulled her jacket closed. I hiked up my tights.

Sheff knelt beside me, whispering, "I don't like him."

"How come?"

"I'll tell you later."

I gulped down another bourbon and ginger. Genevieve said, "Gloria is going to see the Mutoscope exhibit with me."

Paul said, "I'll see it again."

"You weren't invited."

Sheff said, "My stomach's off. I'm going to call it a night."

"It's early," Paul said.

Genevieve said, "Paul can walk you to the train."

"I got it."

"I should go too."

"Nonsense," Genevieve said, sitting up straighter. "Don't do that, Gloria. Stay." She reached out, putting her hand on my thigh. I wanted to stay, but I didn't want to ditch Sheff, not with how much he'd been drinking lately. Sheff grabbed our bottle.

"We have to make plans for the MoMA exhibit," she said.

"Definitely. Just come see me at work."

"When are you working?" She got up when I got up. She was eager, attentive. I liked it.

"Day after tomorrow."

"I'll be there."

As Sheff and I walked toward Columbus Circle, I heard Genevieve and Paul whispering, and I wondered what they were saying. I told Sheff, "I think she likes me."

"You think? She totally digs you."

"I thought Paul would be your type."

"I guess I don't have a type." He hadn't been with anyone but johns since I'd been in New York. "I'm just picky," he added. "Maybe his eyes are too close together."

Back at the hotel, Sheff washed down a Valium with a swig of bourbon. We lay side by side staring at Harry, the jowly water stain. I held *The Catcher in the Rye* on my chest. I'd been reading aloud to Sheff. I said, "Did I tell you that my mother used to be in love with my dad's brother?"

Sheff rolled onto his side. "No! Why do you keep these things from me?" He lit a cigarette.

"It's complicated."

"Complications make for the best stories."

"True."

After I told him all that I knew about my mother and her college boy, he said, "What would you have chosen? The steady Eddie who wasn't Eddie or the wild one, your uncle Eddie?"

"First off, gross! I wouldn't choose my father or my uncle."

"You know what I mean."

He passed me the cigarette. I took a drag, exhaling toward Harry. "I don't know," I said. "I don't know if she really had a choice."

Sheff said, "Growing up sucks. Grown-ups are the worst. We're not going to grow up and be like them." Then he paused. "Do you think you were really in love with Isabel? I mean, do you think that love is a real thing? Romantic love?"

"Yes. I'm pretty sure. I never wanted to be away from her. When she left my house or I had to leave hers, I felt depressed."

"I want to be in love someday."

"You will be."

He crossed his arms at his chest. "I don't think life is going to let me have that."

"Don't say that." I leaned into him, my arm across his chest, the book pressed between us. A few hours later, I awoke to Sheff kicking and punching at nothing, shouting at no one. I tried waking him. "It's okay. Calm down."

But I knew that it wasn't okay. Something was very wrong.

13

Two nights later, we were having drinks at the Big Panda, waiting for a jazz trio to start playing, when a man in his midthirties, shaggy brown hair and green eyes, came to our table. He was younger than the others. I expected him to put a five- or ten-dollar bill on the table, but instead, he sat down.

"What are you looking for?" Sheff asked.

"I want to talk to you." He smiled.

Sheff smiled back, finishing his highball. "What is it you want to talk about?"

From across the table, I half waved. I had no idea who this man was or what he wanted.

"My name's Brian Biden. I knew Chuck before he moved back to Maryland."

I looked at Sheff. "Who's Chuck?"

"Sal Mineo . . . ," Sheff explained. "Chuck was his real name."

"Got it."

Then, Sheff looked up at Brian Biden. "I've got nothing to say to you."

"Just five minutes." Brian straddled a chair.

"I don't want to talk to you." Sheff brushed his hair back from his face. He was noticeably upset.

"He doesn't want to talk to you," I said.

"Look, Sheff," Brian began, "I'm working on a grant for the University of California at Berkeley. I want to help. Chuck told me about Belmont. I'm not here to harass you."

Sheff said, "I don't care what Chuck told you. He was a head case."

Brian shook his head, his voice lower. "I really think I can help."

"Just leave me the fuck alone." Sheff reached for his drink, his hand shaking.

Brian got up and pulled a card from his wallet, extending it to Sheff, who said, "No, thanks." Brian handed it to me. He sighed before walking away.

"Why'd you take his card?" Sheff asked.

"Who was that? What happened with Sal Mineo?"

Sheff opened his hand, waiting for me to give him Brian's business card. I placed it on his palm. "Thanks." He tore the card into little pieces, sprinkling the paper in the ashtray. "Fuck that guy."

"Who is he?"

"He's some kind of head doctor like Dr. Belmont, except he's the opposite. I mean, he doesn't think there's anything wrong with being queer. Chuck swallowed some of his psychotherapy bullshit before he split town."

"What exactly happened with Sal Mineo? You never told me."

"Chuck."

"Right. What happened with Chuck?"

"I don't want to talk about it, Gloria."

"It seems like something we should talk about."

"Nope."

An older man approached our table, his five-dollar bill in hand.

"I'm going back to the hotel," I said.

"Suit yourself."

If Sheff wouldn't confide in me, then who would he confide in?

On the sidewalk outside the Big Panda, Brian appeared from around the corner. "Can you please listen to me for a second?"

I glanced back to see if Sheff had followed. He hadn't.

Brian said, "Listen, Chuck told me what they did to Sheff at Belmont." Bats crisscrossed the streetlight. "I think I can help him."

"What did they do to him?"

"They messed with his head."

"They messed with mine too."

"Okay," Brian said, folding his arms at his chest. "I'll be more specific. From what I understand, Dr. Belmont rewired Sheff's brain."

"I don't understand."

"Ask Sheff. Just ask him, and see what he says. He needs help." He handed me another card. "I can get him help. Have him call me."

I slipped the card in my bag and walked home alone.

When Sheff stumbled in at three, he was plastered. He mumbled something about "stupid Brian Biden" before passing out with one boot on, one off. I brushed the hair back from his forehead and kissed his hairline. Then, I went to sleep. I knew that we were going to pretend that everything was all right. That's just what we did.

By the end of December, Sheff was taking tranquilizers on a daily basis to keep himself calm. He couldn't seem to drink enough to pass out, and when he did sleep, he sweated so profusely that we had to buy extra sheets and blankets from the Salvation Army. Then, he started getting up in the middle of the night and going down the hall to the bathroom to vomit. His face was sallow. Raccoon eyes. I went to the Mutoscope show with Genevieve and spent one night in her dorm, but I worried about Sheff. It was getting harder to pretend that everything was okay.

One morning as we were changing the sheets, I couldn't keep quiet any longer. It was early January. Sheff and I had been living together since late August. As I popped the bed-sheet, a cold gust of wind swept up the street, rattling the broken French door. I said, "Tell me the truth. What's going on with you? You're not eating, you're not sleeping. You're not dating any Hollywood look-alikes. And what really happened with Sal Mineo? Why was that Brian guy bugging you?"

"Chuck." Sheff pulled at the bedsheet in my hands. "I'm fine."

"Right, Chuck." We held the sheet, the mattress between us. Sheff took a deep breath. "I don't want to talk about it."

"Please talk to me." Then I realized I already knew the truth. I'd simply refused to face it. I crawled onto the mattress, the sheet still in my hands, and looked up at him. "You did it. That's how you got out. You did that therapy."

Sheff let go of the sheet. His eyes were bloodshot. He ran one hand through his hair, gripping the ends. "You're worse than fucking Chuck or Biden," he said.

"Did you tell him? Did you tell Chuck? Did you tell Brian Biden?" I heard Sheff's stomach rumbling. He couldn't keep anything down. Our room smelled of stale liquor, sweat, and smoke. I opened one of the French doors. The cold wind whipped through the room. The flower pot was still out there, clanking against the railing.

Sheff said, "I don't want to keep things from you. After you got here, I felt better. I thought I would keep getting better."

"What happened?"

"I did it. I did the PERVERSION therapy." His hands

were in fists. "You were gone, and I just wanted to get out of there."

I closed the French door and leaned against it. Was this somehow my fault? I reached for him.

"Don't touch me."

"I'm sorry."

He was trembling. "So, basically they did this thing where they put me in a cinder block room, a drain in the middle of the floor, and they showed films of men masturbating and having sex with each other, but first, they give me an injection that made me physically sick so that the whole time I was watching the pornography, I was violently ill. When I tried to look away, they strapped me to a chair. They strapped my fucking head to a chair and taped my eyelids open." He paused. "I threw up and shit myself." His hands shook as he knocked a cigarette from his pack with one already burning in the ashtray. "Later, they came in and hosed me off. And they kept doing this until I begged them to stop. The whole time, they're telling me that the therapy is working because I'm totally sick, groveling and crying, and the films never stopped rolling. Even now, when I close my eyes or stop doing shit for one second, when it's time to be still and sleep, it comes back to me. Fuck, Gloria! I can't just be. I can't be." He sat on the bed, pulling his knees to his chest. "I knew that they wouldn't let me out if I didn't do the therapy, but I didn't know how awful it would be."

"I shouldn't have left you in there."

"You couldn't have gotten me out. No one could. No one

except for Dr. Belmont or Pop. They got what they wanted. I can't use my dick."

I reached out to hold him, and this time, he let me get close. I took him in my arms and squeezed. He whispered, "There was a bed beside the chair where I slept; it was stainless steel. It always sounded like a train in my head, a rumbling. It hurt and it never stopped. I had thought it was a good idea. I thought I could handle anything, and when I agreed to do the aversion therapy, my pop said that he was proud of me. He said that I was showing real promise. I just needed to get out of there, G."

I wanted to take his pain away, but I couldn't. I was helpless. "I'm so sorry." I pictured Dr. Belmont in his silver-rimmed spectacles. We needed to undo what he'd done. I held Sheff tight. "So, what about Brian Biden?" I still had his card. "Can he help you?"

"He says that they can fix me. I told him, I've already been fixed. I've been fucking neutered." Sheff half laughed, half cried.

"You can't keep living like this."

"The thing is," he said, "I don't think anyone can undo what was done to me."

"But if there's a chance . . . You have a chance."

"That would be something," he said, "if I could get better. If I could stop having nightmares. But it sounds like I'd have to go to Berkeley, and it probably wouldn't help anyway."

"You have to try."

The next afternoon, we met Brian in Washington Square Park. We sat on a stone bench. I blew on my hands to keep them warm. Sheff wore his peacoat, the collar upturned. Brian wore a leather jacket. He said, "I'm really proud of you, Sheff, for telling Gloria the truth." Brian turned to me. "He didn't want you to think he was weak."

"Right, because they broke me or something. I'm all fucked up." Sheff rolled his eyes and lit a cigarette.

Brian took a deep breath, regarding Sheff with a mixture of pity and frustration. "You can pretend whatever you want. You can pretend it's no big deal, that you weren't tortured, but we both know the truth. Our current medical system is supporting the hypothesis that homosexuality is a medical illness and, thus, a condition that can be treated and reversed. And, as in your case, innocent men and women are being tortured. I'm on a grant team that is studying the long- and short-term effects of institutions like Belmont on the human psyche."

"Did something like this happen to you?" I asked Brian. "Is that why you're doing this?"

"No. My parents have always supported me. Of course, they're a minority. Sadly."

"So, what's in Berkeley?" I asked.

"Sheff," he said, "hopefully. And you're welcome too."

I had already decided that I was going wherever Sheff was

going. If I had to call Gwen Babineaux or Uncle Eddie and beg them for the money, I'd do it. I wasn't leaving Sheff's side.

Sheff said, "I like New York. I don't want to go to the West Coast."

"Our room has roaches and mice, darling."

"They're nice-enough roaches."

"Oh, come on."

Sheff said, "What if it doesn't work?"

"Nothing ventured, nothing gained."

"I don't like doctors. I'm doing pretty good here."

I shook my head. "No, you're not."

Sheff got up and walked toward the pretzel vendor.

Brian turned to me, "I think the doctors at UC Berkeley can help him. Of course, there are no guarantees."

"Let me talk to him."

Sheff was ordering three pretzels. I sidled up to him. "I thought you wanted to give this a try. I thought you wanted to get better."

"I don't want to be a guinea pig anymore."

"This will be different."

"How?"

"They want to let you be the hard-dicked Sheff you used to be."

Sheff laughed.

"You're scared," I said. "It's okay to be scared. We're in this together. I'll be with you."

Sheff looked at me. "Are you sure?"

"Of course."

He took the pretzels from the vendor. "It'll be cool to see the sun set over the ocean."

"And I don't think they have mosquitoes on the West Coast."

"That's reason enough to go. Are you sure you want to go? What about your parents? You miss them."

"I'll talk to them. They'll be cool . . . You'll see."

"Then let's do it."

We walked back to the bench. Sheff handed Brian a pretzel. "I'm in."

Brian smiled and began to explain the details. "I'll get you the bus tickets. Once you get to Berkeley, our grant chair, Dr. Reginald Cosley, will set you up with a place to stay. He'll have release forms for you to sign. The forms just say that you consent to counseling and therapy and that you're willing to have your data recorded, anonymously, of course."

Sheff set his pretzel down, leaning back on the stone bench, slipping his smokes from his jeans pocket. He pulled the cellophane tab to open the pack and put a cigarette to his lips.

Brian continued, "I'll write everything down for you."

I squeezed Sheff's thigh.

Brian asked, "Are you two good with this?"

We were going cross-country like Kerouac. "Yes." We spoke at the same time.

That night, we went out for pancakes. Outside our window, a neon pink sign buzzed *Pancakes and Pies.* Sheff quoted Holden Caulfield: "'Only, I didn't eat the doughnuts. I couldn't swallow them too well. The thing is, if you get very depressed about something, it's hard as hell to swallow.'" Then, he shoved a forkful of pancakes in his mouth. For once, it was easy to swallow.

14

WE WOKE TO THE CACOPHONOUS bang of the dumpster being emptied. I crawled out of bed, my breath visible. I needed to pick up my last paycheck from Bart's Vinyl and send a postcard to my parents. I nudged Sheff. "I'm going."

He sat up. "It's freezing."

"Good thing we're going west, young man!"

"Will you get me a bagel?"

"You bet, but get up. Pack."

Sheff rolled over.

"I'm serious."

The worst things in the world happen on an upswing with no forewarning. I was a block from the hotel when I saw the barricade. There were three police cars, a fire truck, and an ambulance parked in the middle of the street. I was holding the bag with Sheff's bagel.

Inside the hotel, Clark, the front desk clerk, ran up to me. "It's Sheff," he said. "He jumped. I'm so sorry."

"What are you talking about?"

Clark pointed me out to two gray-suited detectives. He said again, "I'm so sorry. His dad came to get him. Something happened."

"I have his bagel." I headed for the stairs. He had to be up there in bed still asleep, waiting on me.

The gray-suited detectives stopped me before I made the stairs. Sheff would say, *What took you so long? Did you get sesame? I'm starving.* The detectives steered me toward the green velveteen sofa, where I sat with the bagel on my lap. We weren't going to be Kerouac. We weren't going to see the sun set over the Pacific. He wasn't going to be cured. He wasn't going to be happy. I had bus tickets. I had Brian Biden's card. I had the phone number for Dr. Cosley in Berkeley. I had things of no use to anyone.

"Can you tell us your name?"

I didn't answer.

They asked Clark, "What's her name?"

"Gloria."

"Gloria, you need to cooperate with us. We think your friend committed suicide."

"He wouldn't do that."

"He was a runaway. His father came for him this morning. He'd apparently had some mental health problems."

"His father came for him?"

"How old are you?"

I was older than everyone then.

"We need to telephone your parents. They'll need to pick you up at the station." But it wouldn't be Sheff. He wouldn't kill himself, wouldn't be gone, couldn't be gone.

One of the detectives said, "I feel so bad for the kid's father. He finally tracks him down, and the kid jumps off a roof."

I could see it. I could imagine how it played out.

Pop Schoeffler paid the fifty-cent toll and drove through the Lincoln Tunnel, mindful that he was beneath the Hudson River. On the drive, he thought about the multitude of times his son had embarrassed him. He planned to tell his son, You won't embarrass me again. You're my only son. It's time to start acting like it.

As Pop took a right on Ninth Avenue, he felt confident that he would be returning to New Jersey with his son. He noticed a flock of blackbirds, hundreds of them perched on the roof of the Church of the Holy Apostles at 28th. He'd never seen so many birds. They lined the cross-shaped tran-

septs for two city blocks. As Pop crossed 25th Street, the birds ascended, trailing his black Corvette.

Pop took a left onto 23rd Street, the birds coasting. Pop parked in front of the Chelsea as the birds alighted on its roof, pecking and nudging for space. On the sidewalk, Sheff was buttoning his peacoat, sliding his hands in his pockets.

A little girl wearing a sky blue cape and matching gloves ate an Oreo and kicked a pebble on the sidewalk at the corner of 23rd and Seventh Avenue. Her older brother swung from a rattling fire escape while their mother, oblivious, searched through her handbag for subway tokens.

Pop, smiling at the sky-blue girl, slipped his hands into his pockets. Cigarette butts, white like chalk, crisscrossed the sidewalk. The mother was disheveled, the hem of her pink waitress uniform visible under her coat. She wore square-toed black heels.

The sky-blue girl smiled back at Pop while her rough-and-tumble brother continued to swing from the fire escape. Pop was trailing Sheff, calling his name.

Sheff began to trot.

"I've come to take you home."

Sheff said, "Go away."

Pop pointed back toward the Chelsea. "My car's just back there."

Across the street, a blue jay alighted on a stone gargoyle.

"Where are you going?" Pop asked.

"Not your concern."

"A boy doesn't outrun his father."

Sheff lit a cigarette, slipping his hands in his pockets, his sandy-blond hair falling over his eyes, the cigarette dangling from his lips, and he tossed his head back to get a good look at his pop, to show him that he was nearly grown.

"You've had your fun," Pop said. "It's time to come home."

Sheff didn't say anything. He'd learned that there was no point.

"I'm not asking," Pop said. "I'm telling."

Then, Sheffield Schoeffler ran. He did not run for the subway, which was right there at the corner of Eighth and 23rd. He ran east. Sheff pulled down the fire escape ladder where the little boy had been playing, and he climbed up toward the blue sky and the birds. When he reached the roof, he saw six gargoyles across the street. They had maniacal faces, pointed ears, and dragon's wings. They were observing Sheff as he observed them. They saw a young man who was tired of running from his father and the rest of the world.

On the street below, the waitress mother, finding her subway tokens, screamed for her children to "Get over here right now." A hot dog vendor was assembling his cart, setting up shop for the day, for the men who would come north from the meatpacking plants to eat hot dogs with chili and mustard and relish for lunch.

The little girl in the sky-blue cape ignored her mother's

command and pointed upward at the birds now singing and chirping, perched on the gargoyles, a sundry of calls.

On the roof, Sheff pulled his smokes from his coat pocket and hunched, blocking the wind, to light one, to figure out how he was going to shake his old man, once and for all.

Below, the waitress applied her lipstick and, seeing her son on the fire escape ladder, called to him, "Billy, get down from there."

Sheff inhaled deeply, watching the cherry burn red. His father followed him onto the roof. "I'm so tired of your shit," Pop said. Sheff pulled on his smoke, the ash growing. Then he turned and walked like there was no ledge. No fear.

Sheff was a boy who could not bend, a boy who had already been broken. He walked on air because there was no place left to run. The gargoyles were stone, perched forever on that roof, but the birds saw Sheff. The youthful cardinal, the wise raven, the protective jay, the chirping grackles, all saw, and they disbelieved that a boy could fly.

This was how I imagined Sheff's end. This was how I would one day write it. No happy ending. I knew what the birds knew. Boys don't fly.

Technically, Sheff died from a cracked skull, eight snapped ribs, two shattered wrists, and a fractured pelvis and spine. But I knew the real cause.

Sheff died because I'd left him at Belmont. Sheff died because we should've left sooner for California. Sheff died because you can only fight so hard for so long until you run out of fight.

☙

When the detective said, "The boy's father followed him onto the roof. He was worried for his safety," I bent forward and vomited on the lime shag carpeting. I waited for the bees, but they didn't come. I remained there, hunched over, bile between my boots.

Clark ran over with a rag.

I felt one of the detective's hands on my forearm and tried shaking it off. "We're not done talking."

"He wasn't on drugs."

One of the suits said, "Are we taking her to the station?"

"Her parents have been contacted. They're on their way here. Besides, from what Walter Schoeffler said, it sounds like suicide."

I couldn't catch my breath. Clark was down on his knees, cleaning up my puke.

I lost consciousness, waking with my mother on one side of me, my father on the other. When I opened my eyes, my mother kissed my forehead. "They just have a few more questions, and then we can take you home."

One of the suits sat across from us in an orange bucket chair. His jacket was gray. His eyes were brown. His shoes black. I noticed everything about him for the first time. He spoke to my father, "We want to let Miss Ricci go home, but she hasn't been exactly forthright."

"She will be," my mother said.

"We searched their room," he said.

"Their room?" my mother asked.

"They were living together in a one-bedroom." He pulled a cellophane wrapper from a paper envelope. "We found these."

"His Valium," I said.

"It's a depressant."

"He didn't kill himself."

My dad put his arm around me. "Is it all right if we take her home now?"

The detective whispered, "You might want to take her to see somebody, get her professional help."

The other one said, "We'll be in touch."

On the way out, I turned back. "You should know that he was the best person I ever knew. You should write that down."

My father pulled me in tighter. "Let's get you out of here."

15

I WAS IN THE BACK of my dad's new Chrysler, my parents whispering. I said, "I sent postcards." Then, I fell silent. It didn't matter what I said. I had nothing more to give. The police had told my parents their version of events, or Pop's version. They painted Sheff as someone with a mental illness, as someone with a drug addiction. Sheff's sole illness was his father. He'd been born to the wrong family, maybe to the wrong world.

I stared ahead at the seat back, my knees pressed together, every muscle in my body taut. Why couldn't Pop have left him alone? Why couldn't Pop have come a week or even a day later? Then, my mother said, "I feel terrible for that young man's family."

I punched the car door, bruising my fist.

My mother spun around, both hands on the seat back. "Gloria! Stop that!"

"Fuck them! He was never good enough for them!" I fell silent again. No one spoke.

When we pulled into the driveway, I got out of the car. I stared at our squat suburban home, the black mulch where the flowers had died, the cold brown earth, and I dropped to my knees, then to my palms, then to my chest. I wanted to sink into the dirt. My parents watched, speechless.

From the walkway, my mother said, "Come on inside, Gloria," but I remained there.

My father said, "You'll catch your death."

The irony wasn't lost on me. I remained where I was.

A while later, my hands and face numb, I heard Gwen's voice above me. "All right," she said. "You're home now." My body was limp, but she managed to lift me up from under my arms, my knees dragging the ground. She called for my father, and together, they dragged me into the house.

Once indoors, I stripped down naked. My father turned away. My mother said, "Why are you doing this?" Gwen ran for a towel. I followed Gwen into the bathroom, moving past her to the shower, my clothes in a heap in the living room. She said, "You're going to be all right. It's going to get better." I turned the water as hot as I could stand. "I'll be in the den with your parents." The water beat down on my head, and I told God that I didn't believe in him anymore. *Fuck you, God! Fuck you! What kind of god kills all the best people?!*

I stayed in the shower until the water turned cold. Then, I wrapped myself in a towel and stepped into the hallway.

I could hear my parents and Gwen whispering in the den. Hearing me, my parents came down the hall. It was obvious that they didn't know what to say. There was nothing they could say. I went to my bedroom and put on my nightgown. I lay facedown, wishing I could rewind time. Then wishing I could sleep. A while later, my mother climbed in bed beside me. She lay on her side and tried to rest her hand on my head. I knocked it away. I expected her to get up and leave, but she remained.

Eventually, I slept.

The next day, my mother brought me a sandwich and a glass of milk. I wouldn't eat. I couldn't eat. She said, "I love you," and I didn't say anything. Hours passed, and then days. I ate a piece of dry toast every morning, but little else. Then, I remember my mother in bed beside me, one hand on the top of my head. She said, "I'm sorry about your friend. He must have been an amazing person."

I didn't speak, but her words meant so much.

"I know that if you loved him, I would've loved him."

I felt a lump in my throat. I spoke, "He was great."

"What should I know about him?"

So many memories rushed back, but I said, "We were going to have the most beautiful children in the world." I didn't plan on crying, but I cracked. My dam broke. The pain came like a river. "He didn't want to die."

I tucked my head between my knees. "He died." My whole body trembled. "I loved him."

My mother held me. "Let it out."

My father brought a box of Kleenex.

The days had no beginnings and no ends. I slept between bursts of sadness and rage. Sometimes, I was awake at three in the morning. Sometimes I was asleep at two in the afternoon. Everything blurred together.

A week after I was home, Uncle Eddie came to my room. He sat in the window seat, the frost lining the glass. He said, "I had this shrink out west after the war who told me that I needed to burn the things that hurt me."

I thought about Brian Biden's business card. I'd never told Brian that we weren't going to Berkeley. I wondered if anyone had told him. Of course, he would hear about it. Someone at the Big Panda would tell him. Uncle Eddie kept talking. "The idea is that you burn everything that you associate with your pain so you can be free of it. It's like a purging. I brought you some matches." I pulled a match from the box and struck it, using the flame to light a cigarette.

"Did you do this?" I asked. "Did you burn something, and did it help you?"

"Well, yes and no. I mean that I did burn some things, but it didn't help."

"What happened?"

"I wanted the things I burned to come back. I wished I hadn't burned them. But that's me. I'm a fucking wreck. And this is you. Is there anything that you want to burn? It should be something that you won't want to have back. Obviously."

I wanted to burn myself, a big funeral pyre. All I'd done all week was replay Sheff's last day, that last morning we were together, the number of things I could've done to change the outcome, how Sheff must've felt when he saw his pop.

Uncle Eddie and I went to the carport for a cardboard box. I liked the idea of a fire, but I wasn't going to burn anything having to do with Sheff. Rather, I collected my old notebooks, the story about Joan of Arc, everything I'd ever written, and I dumped all of it into the box. I had the letter Isabel had written and some records she'd given me. I'd burn those too. Eddie and I sat in the backyard like a couple of Boy Scouts, a pile of sticks and the box of matches between us. I scraped my nails against the red sulfur tips and snapped one in two before glancing up at him. He said, "You're kind of fucked up, aren't you?"

"I'm all right," I lied. I piled my composition books, notes from Isabel, and the records she'd given me in a heap and lit the match. The smoke rose between us. I knew my parents were watching from the sliding glass door. As the notebook pages burned, their edges blackened and curled. They smoldered orange, the heat creeping page to page, while the vinyl records folded in on themselves, releasing a noxious smell. The darkness came up from the grass and simultaneously down from the clouds. I looked to see my parents at the sliding glass door, but they'd gone. Eddie sprayed the fire with lighter fluid, the flames leaping into the blackness, everything burning faster. The fire was hypnotic and warm. Right then, it was helping. I lay on my side, the sparks illuminating Uncle Eddie's face. He said, "Time will help, Gloria. It makes things easier." I didn't respond. I didn't know what I was going to do, how I'd go on, but I figured I had little choice in the matter. As the fire burned down, the paper floated up, raining ash over our heads.

Later, I woke with Uncle Eddie gone, the fire out, my father helping me to my feet. He guided me indoors and back down the hall to my room. I got into bed and rolled to face the wall. The tears were coming back. My father patted my shoulder. "You're tough, sweetheart." He stayed there all night, rubbing my back, whispering assurances.

He and my mother held vigil those first few months. It was like they were afraid that I was going to take my life. Their fear was unnecessary. I felt that it had already been taken.

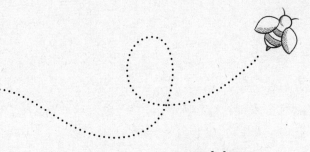

part two

This is the story of America. Everybody's doing what they think they're supposed to do.

—Jack Kerouac, *On the Road*

16

AFTER GRADUATING HIGH SCHOOL, I got a job at Bink's
Department Store downtown as the tie girl. Each morning and
evening, I meticulously cleaned the glass top. I organized the
plaids and Kelly greens, the limes, chartreuses, cherry prints,
cotton-poly blends and silks. Everything was in order. Four
years and three months had passed since Sheff's death. The
world felt unsafe, but within my glass cubicle, I was protected.

Monday through Saturday, I sold neckties, ascots, bow ties,
and cravats. Cravats were my favorite because they were mostly
bought by the older set, retired gentlemen who knew what
they wanted. They were my easiest customers.

After work, I went home. Mother, Father, and I ate together, watching the evening news with Walter Cronkite.
Vietnam was on fire. All the leaders of the civil rights move-

ment had been murdered, and the National Organization for Women was calling for the ratification of the Equal Rights Amendment. On Fridays after work, I went to Gwen's. We drank martinis. My mother started taking classes at a community college. Then one evening after she got home, she said, "Can I talk to you?"

We sat at the kitchen table. She unpacked her notebooks. She had homework, a pile of text and library books.

"What is it?" I asked.

"You're hiding."

I shrugged. "I don't know what you mean."

"Why don't you get a job in the city? Get out of Maryville. Live a little."

"I'm fine how I am."

"I'm worried about you."

"Don't be." I left her at the table with her schoolwork.

The next afternoon, I met a man as dark as Sheff had been fair. Dark hair. Dark eyes. He stood a little slouched, his hands deep in his pockets, glancing up as I sold a bow tie to a young woman. After the young woman left my department, he remained. I walked over to the jewelry department and asked my coworker Cora, "Is that man looking over here?"

"The good-looking one?" Cora was funny. She was always husband hunting.

"I don't know."

"He is. Now he's walking toward the tie counter." She smiled. "You better get over there. Maybe he's rich."

He was waiting for me. "Hello. How can I help you?"

"I don't know if you can," he said. His fingers were spread wide, smudging my countertop.

"Are you interested in a particular cut or color?"

He had thick eyelashes and brown eyes. "Actually, I'm interested in you."

The brashness was familiar. "Excuse me?"

"I like you," he said.

"You don't know me."

"But I could get to know you." He smiled. "Go out with me."

"I think not."

"If I buy a tie, will you go out with me?"

"No."

"I'll buy five ties."

I cracked a smile. "Do you need a necktie?"

"As much as any guy needs a noose, but that doesn't matter."

"Of course it matters. If you don't need a tie, you shouldn't buy one."

He leaned across the countertop. "Which ones do you like?"

"It doesn't matter."

"Show me your favorites."

"Why?"

"Please."

I slid the case open and pulled out my favorite Italian silk ascots. "Feel this," I said.

He rubbed at the yellow silk, but kept his eyes on me. "Do you like spaghetti? There's an Italian place just down the street. I like spaghetti."

"Why me? Why not bother someone else?" I asked.

"Why not you? The blonde curls. The blue eyes. Your smile. I was in here last week buying some boxer shorts, and I saw you, and I knew that I had to come back and ask you out."

Sheff had once said, *If you're not living, you're dying.* "What's the name of the Italian place?"

"Gino's."

"I know it. I could meet you there."

"I want to buy the ascot."

"No, you don't."

"Sure, I do."

"You really don't." I showed him the price tag.

"I really don't. But something else. Something for our date. You pick."

"It's not really a date."

"Sure it is."

I chose a thin blue tie, a cotton-poly blend, nothing too fancy, nothing too expensive.

He said, "Is seven good?"

I nodded. Then, I saw Cora waving her arms to get my attention. She pointed at him, fanning herself, feigning fainting. I laughed. He looked back to see Cora.

"Who's that?"

"Cora. She works in jewelry."

He waved back. "So, I'll meet you there."

"Okay."

"Great. See you at seven." He tapped the counter with both hands and turned to go.

"Wait. You don't know my name."

"You're wearing a name tag, Miss Gloria Ricci."

"Then I don't know yours."

"Jacob Blount."

"Pleased to meet you."

"I'll see you tonight."

As he walked away, Cora rushed to my counter. "What does he do?" she asked.

"I don't know what he does."

"Did he ask you out?"

"He did."

"What did you say?"

"Yes."

When I got to Gino's, Jacob was already seated. There was a red votive on the checkered tablecloth. He wore a white button-down oxford, the blue tie I'd picked out, and faded jeans. His face was clean-shaven, and his dark hair was combed back in a pompadour. Seeing me, he got to his feet, an eagerness in his stance. "You look really pretty."

"Thank you," I said.

We sat in silence for a minute before I asked, "What is it that you're doing here in Maryville?"

"That's a very good question." He leaned back, packing his cigarettes on the table. "They call it construction, building roads and houses, but it's destruction. It's ripping roots out of the ground to make way for greedy consumers, men who like to buy cravats and ascots, no offense to you. It's destroying all that is good, everything green." He pulled hard on his cigarette. "As soon as my job ends, I'm getting out of here. It's going to sound strange, but I think I came here to find you. You ever feel that way about things, like you're not in control, like someone else is at the steering wheel? As soon as I saw you, I said, 'I have to meet her.'"

My palms were sweating. He had no idea how much that resonated with me. I'd spent my whole life feeling like someone else was at the steering wheel. I lit a cigarette.

"I'm a purist," he continued.

"Meaning?"

"It means that I won't buy what the man is selling. I'm tired of making zilch for working my ass off so somebody else can get fat and rich and drive a fancy car."

"But what will you do for work?" I asked.

"I don't know, but I know it'll be big."

We were interrupted by the waitress, who had brought our food. Jacob had ordered spaghetti Bolognese. He slurped the noodles up while I wound mine around my fork. We split a bottle of Chianti, and he talked a blue streak, how Sheff used to do, about his future plans. He was twenty-seven, a bit of a vagabond, he admitted, but ready to plant roots. "I'm moving back to North Carolina," he said, "as soon as I finish this job. I need funds."

I drank the Chianti down.

"I'm going to start my own business, like a salvage business. I'm going to collect what other men throw away, and I'm going to make gold from their garbage." I finished my wine, and Jacob refilled my glass. "But I'm in town a while longer, and I met this beautiful girl, and she went to dinner with me, so I'm in no hurry to go anywhere."

"Oh, really."

"Yes, really. In fact, she seems damn near perfect except for the fact that she sells nooses."

"I like what I do."

He reached across the table, putting his hand on mine. "To each his own, but it seems like you're better than a job like that . . . If you ask me."

"I could never figure out what I wanted to do."

"Life's short. You better start figuring."

We clinked our glasses.

It was past nine when we left the restaurant. Jacob walked me to my car. His hair had flopped down over his eyes, and without thinking, I swept it back. He smiled.

It started to drizzle. My back was against the car. I dug into my clutch for my keys. He was staring at me. The rain was picking up. I was nervous that he was going to try and kiss me, so I extended my hand. He laughed. "Can I see you again?"

"Sure."

"Can I pick you up so it's an official date?" He seemed to have no pretense. *Sheff.*

"Okay."

"Can I get your address and phone number so that I'll be able to pick you up?"

I was wet. "Okay."

"You're very agreeable, Gloria Ricci."

"I have a pen," I said. "I'll write my address and phone number down." I reached inside my clutch again, the cold rain coming down harder.

"Just tell me. I'll remember. If I hear something I want to remember, I don't forget."

I told him my phone number and address. "I live with my parents."

"Nice."

Then, I slipped down into the driver's seat, adrenaline streaming into my limbs, and Jacob shut my door. He took a step back. It was pouring. The wind had picked up, blowing the rain in sheets. I started the engine and turned on the windshield wipers. He stood there, the rain pelting him, his white shirt sticking to his undershirt. As I drove away, I glanced in the rearview mirror to see him still standing there.

When I got home, my parents were up. My mother said,

"Did you have a good time? Were you out with Cora?" I'd only told them that I was meeting friends for dinner. My father was sitting in his recliner, eating buttered saltines.

"I went on a date."

My father righted his recliner. My mother said, "What do you mean when you say that you went on a date?" She whispered, "With a woman?"

"His name is Jacob Blount. I met him at work."

"Who is he?" my mother asked.

My father said, "I was under the impression that you didn't date."

"I don't know," I said. "He's funny."

"What does he do for a living?" my father asked.

"He's a purist." I walked toward my bedroom, my parents following.

"What's a purist?" my father wanted to know. He leaned against the doorjamb, my mother at his side.

I slipped off my shoes. "I met him in the tie department, but he doesn't like ties. He calls them nooses."

My father said, "I've never heard of a purist."

"You'll meet him. He's picking me up tomorrow night."

At ten forty-five, the telephone rang. I could hear my father asking, "Do you know what time it is?" and then I heard his slippers in the hall. He pushed open my door. "It's that man you were telling us about, the purist, on the phone. I told him that some of us traditionalists work for a living, but that I'd check to see if you were awake."

"I'm awake." I got out of bed and, passing by my father, kissed his cheek. "I'll take it in the kitchen."

I picked up the receiver. "I've got it, Dad. You can hang up now."

Jacob said, "It's me."

"Hi, me."

"I was thinking about you."

"I was thinking about you." I twisted the phone cord around my arm.

"Are we still on for tomorrow night?"

"Sure. Do you still remember my address?"

"Sure do."

"Then, we're on," I said.

"I just wanted to hear your voice before I went to sleep."

It was the damnedest thing. I liked a man.

17

THE NEXT NIGHT, THERE WAS a tuna-noodle casserole on the
table. My father was drinking a gin fizz, and my mother was
scurrying, emptying ashtrays, and straightening my father's
magazines. She cleared off the countertop, putting her school
things in a tote bag. Father said, "What does he do again?"

"Construction, I think, but he wants to be a purist."

"Right," my father said. "Gotta love purity."

"So, he wears a hard hat?" my mother asked.

"I guess." I sat on the sofa in a pink miniskirt, knocking my
knees, waiting for seven o'clock.

My mother said, "And he's a man, and you like him?"

"I think," I said.

Mother said, "I told Gwen about him. If you still like him
tomorrow, she wants to meet him."

"We'll see how it goes."

The doorbell rang. My parents shadowed me to the door. Jacob wore a button-down pin-striped shirt and blue jeans. No tie. He had his hands in his pockets. It was a warm April, and beyond him, I could see the honeybees flitting from pansy to hyacinth to tulip. I said, "This is Jacob. Jacob, these are my parents."

My mother said, "I'm Molly. It's nice to meet you. Please come in."

My father said, "Good to meet you. Can I interest you in a gin fizz?"

Jacob said, "That sounds refreshing." He shook my father's hand. Then, he took hold of mine and squeezed. It felt strange, but nice. We followed my dad to the kitchen.

"Where are you two going tonight?" my mother asked.

"Maybe see a movie," Jacob said. "I thought I'd check with Gloria."

"I can check the paper for the times," my mother said.

"You know, I've never had a gin fizz," Jacob said.

Father began slicing lemons at the counter while Jacob and I sat at the dining room table.

"I just made a casserole. Would you like some?"

"No, thank you."

My mother said, "So Gloria tells us you're working construction."

"Yes, ma'am. I'm repaving Route 6 out in Burrus."

"Do you like it?"

"Not really, but it's a job."

"And where are you from?"

Father said, "Don't be nervous, Jacob. Molly's not the grand inquisitor. She just acts like it sometimes."

"Very funny, Frank."

"I'm from a small town in southeast North Carolina. It's about a two-hour drive from Raleigh, if you've ever been there."

"I've never been," my mother said.

"Me either," Father said. He was at the counter, adding gin, sugar, and ice to the tumbler. "Nothing better than a good fizz." He shook the concoction.

Mother said, "What's the name of the town?"

"It's really Podunk," Jacob said, "called Greeley, sometimes spelled with an extra 'e' and sometimes spelled without, depending on who you ask or where you are in town."

My father laughed.

"It's pretty funny," Jacob said. "There's not much there, so I thought I'd work construction and travel around some."

Father brought our drinks over. "Did you go to college, Jacob? Molly just started taking classes."

Jacob said, "No, sir, I didn't go to college, but I've thought about that, and I'm only twenty-seven. I might go still. There's no telling what I'll do. The world is full of possibility."

Mother said, "And you're calling me the grand inquisitor . . ."

We finished our drinks, and Jacob shook my father's hand.

"Thank you for letting Gloria come out with me. She won't be home late."

In the driveway, I climbed into Jacob's powder-blue Chevy truck. There was a pile of empty cigarette packages between us, empty beer cans at my feet. Father and Mother waved from the front stoop. Then, a bee flew in through my window, and Jacob said, "Goddamn it," trying to swat it.

"There's a hive in our backyard."

"You ought to torch it." He smashed the bee on the dashboard, the yellow pollen on his palm. The bee dropped down to the beer cans.

"You didn't have to do that."

He rubbed his hand against his jeans. "You could've been stung."

I was nervous. The beer cans and dead bee didn't sit well. "My mother never looked up the movie times."

"Do you want to see a movie?" he asked.

"I don't know. I guess."

"I have another idea. Is that okay?" He looked at me. "It'll be fun."

"I guess so."

"I want to show you where I live, but don't worry. I don't have any funny business in mind."

As we started driving out of town, I said, "Do you really think you might go to college one day?"

"Hell, no. I was just telling your parents what I knew they wanted to hear. There's nothing any professor can teach me that I don't already know. No offense to any professors. I just don't believe in paying a man who thinks he's smarter than me to tell me things I can learn on my own. What about you? Did you go to college?"

"No."

"You seem pretty smart."

"Thanks."

The sun was setting as we drove by long stretches of barbed wire fencing, barns, and silos. There were cows gathered around watering holes. No houses. No streetlights. The radio station was crackling.

I said, "Where exactly do you live?"

"You'll see."

"We told my parents we wouldn't be out late."

"But old trucks break down all the time." He patted my thigh. "I'm just kidding."

I lit a cigarette. "I'm hungry. Maybe we can get something to eat." I shifted in the seat, hot-boxing my smoke.

He reached over and opened the glove box. "I got a bottle of Seagram's 7 and some peanut-butter crackers."

He had a lean face, sharp cheekbones. He turned the radio dial to a Patsy Cline song, "Walkin' After Midnight," and I sipped the whiskey. I felt a surge of adrenaline. For the past five years, I'd been trying not to live, but then I met Jacob, and so many things were familiar. I wanted to let myself go, feel untethered again, give in to whatever lay ahead.

"I love Patsy," he said.

"She's pretty good."

"We're nearly there." There was a road sign for Route 12 on our right. "It's just down here." He drove along a narrow gravel road, dense oaks on both sides, the low branches dragging the roof and scratching the windows. The sun was setting fast. Jacob pulled up, parking beside a barn. "We're here," he said, opening his door, leaving the keys in the ignition. I was opening my door when he came around to open it for me. He took my hand. I was glad I'd worn flats. It was dark, the ground uneven. I heard screech owls in the trees.

I said, "You're not going to kill me, are you?"

"Yes, Gloria." He stopped walking and turned to face me. "I've brought you out here to murder you. I hope that's okay." His face was deadpan.

"Sure," I said. "Kill away."

He smiled. "You're going to love this." The barn was weathered. An old rusty tractor was parked to its right. Jacob slid the door open, leading me inside. He flipped a light switch.

"Wow!" I said. A golden retriever bounded toward us.

"This is Oscar." The dog sidled up to Jacob.

"From the outside, you'd never guess it was so nice in here." The interior was painted bright yellow. Copper light fixtures hung from the rafters. In the center of the barn, there was a big rustic table, a jar of flowers, a bottle of wine, and two glasses at its center. I saw the dog's bowls beside the table. In the far corner, there were a few motorcycles and some bicycles. In the back of the barn, there was a ladder leading up to a loft.

Jacob said, "I wanted you to meet Oscar. He's my best pal."

I petted the dog. "He's so sweet."

Then, a woman in her midthirties slid the door open. She had a long silver braid hanging over one shoulder. "I have pizza for your date."

Jacob said, "This is Lillian, my landlord. She owns the farm. I'm renting the barn."

"Hi. Nice to meet you." I was still petting Oscar.

Jacob took the pizza from Lillian. "Now, Gloria won't think of me as the guy who hates neckties. She'll think of me as the guy who lives in a barn and has a cool dog."

"And a cool landlord," Lillian said.

"Do you want a slice, Lil?" Jacob asked.

"No, thanks. I'm going to skedaddle."

"Thanks again."

"No problem. Have fun."

As Lillian slid the barn door closed, Jacob poured me a glass of wine. "And you thought I was going to kill you." He laughed.

"Not really."

"I know."

He took my hand and led me to the table. "Can I kiss you?"

"Okay." I was a nervous wreck, but he'd never guess that I'd never kissed a man. I didn't think. I hoped.

He leaned in, and I closed my eyes. His lips were soft, and he slid his hand up the back of my neck under my curls how Sheff used to do. I wanted him to keep his hand there. He said, "That was nice."

"It was."

Oscar curled at Jacob's feet. He passed me a slice.

"So, how do you know Lillian?" I asked.

"She went to school with my sister, Meredith. When she heard that I was looking for work up north, she said I could stay here. Make some money."

"Do you pay rent?"

"Kind of. I help out. Do odd jobs, pitch in when I can. Mostly, I'm saving up to have my own house, my own land."

"Be the purist," I added.

"Exactly . . . You're like your mother. You ask a lot of questions."

"I am."

After we ate, Jacob said, "Do you want to see the loft?"

"What kind of girl do you think I am?"

"No funny business."

"I don't believe you."

"Scout's honor. Unless you throw yourself at me."

"Sure. Why not?" I was living. I was trying.

He said, "You go up the ladder first. That way, if you fall, I'll catch you." He stood just below me as I navigated each rung. When I reached the top, I looked back at him. "Oh, it's really nice."

"This view's not bad either."

"Stop." The flooring was tongue-and-groove, and I was able to stand up easily. There was a bright red-and-orange braided rug and a large mattress covered with a quilt. On both ends of the loft, there were windows, and one of them had a fan that whirred, blowing in the cool night air.

Jacob said, "And now I've got you right where I want you." He rubbed his hands together, laughing, before sitting on the mattress, patting the spot beside him.

I sat. Then, he lay back, his hands behind his head. "When I go home to Greeley, I'm going to get my own land, something like this, something where I can be self-sufficient."

I was perched on my elbows. I didn't have future plans. I'd almost made a point of not making any.

He rolled onto his side, facing me. "What should we do now?"

"I don't know."

"I could kiss you again."

"That's one idea." *I'm living. I should live.*

Down below, Oscar started barking. "Don't mind him," Jacob said. "He can climb up here if he wants. He's done it before." I could see a small bee trapped in a spiderweb by the fan. The spider's back was white and shimmered in the light. Jacob kissed me. *Can I be with a man? I'm with one now.*

Then, he stopped. "We should get you home."

"Didn't you say that old trucks break down all the time?"

Jacob raised his eyebrows. "Good girl gone bad? What do you have in mind?"

"I don't know." I leaned in and kissed him. "I'm kind of new at this."

"I'm not." He straddled me, slipping one hand up my

blouse. I didn't resist. He unhooked my bra. I wasn't aroused, but I was hopeful. Then his hands were under my skirt, and I heard Oscar on the ladder, his nails scratching the wood as he started climbing up to the loft. Then my skirt was up around my waist. Jacob was unbuttoning my blouse, breathing heavily. "Oh, I want you," he said. He pushed my breasts together, putting one in his mouth. Then he looked up at me to see if I was watching. "Does it feel good?" I was excited by how he was looking at me and the way he was talking to me.

"Yes," I said.

"Good."

I forgot my parents. I forgot that I said I wouldn't be out late. I forgot the bee in the web, the dog who was now at my feet. Everything. When he put his mouth between my legs, I grabbed onto his hair. He started laughing. Then, I grabbed onto the sheets. He stopped long enough to ask, "Does it feel good?"

"Yes," I told him. "It feels so good."

The next morning, he drove me home before he had to go to work. The sun was just up. We sat in his truck in my parents' driveway. "Do you want me to walk you to the door?"

"No. I got this."

When I turned the key, I looked back to see Jacob waving, backing out of the driveway. My parents were sitting at the kitchen table, drinking coffee. My mother said, "For all we knew, you were in a ditch."

"His truck broke down, and then there wasn't a phone,

and it was really late, and I didn't want him to drive that late, and he had to work today."

"Since he's a purist, I didn't think a job would matter to him," my father said.

"Well, he has to make some money first to live as a purist."

"Oh boy, Gloria," my father said. "I don't think I like this fellow."

My mother said, "You never go anywhere, and then you stay out all night! With a man . . . It's pretty disconcerting. We don't know what to expect."

"I like him," I said. "That's all."

My parents looked at each other before my mother said, "Make sure you call next time."

"I will. I promise."

18

THE NEXT SATURDAY, JACOB AND I took the train to the Jersey Shore. We'd spent every evening together since we'd met. It was a blustery, cold day. Jacob bought me a candy apple, and we walked along the boardwalk, his arm draped over my shoulder. I hadn't been to the shore since that first week in New York when Sheff and I took the train to Coney Island. Every time we passed a tall blond man, I did a double take. That had been a strange, magical day. I remembered the girl in the mermaid tail and creepy Madame Zelda. She hadn't seen Sheff's fortune.

On the boardwalk, Jacob said, "Do you want to spend the night? I could get a room."

I hesitated, but only for a minute. "Why not? Let's do it." While Jacob went into Tanya's Market for cigarettes, I called my mother from a pay phone. "We're having fun," I said, "so we've decided to spend the night."

"What's going on?" she asked.

"I like him."

"I thought you liked girls."

"Maybe I like both."

"I don't think it's a good idea. Why don't you come home?"

The operator said, "Please deposit ten cents."

"You told me to call. I'm calling."

"I don't know how many times we can say we're sorry about Belmont!"

"This has nothing to do with that." Before the operator disconnected our call, I hung up. Here I was with a man, a man I liked, and she was asking me about girls. I waited for Jacob outside Tanya's. I was putting the past behind me, and she had to bring up Belmont!

"How did it go?" he asked.

"It went."

He put his hand on my shoulder. "Let's ride the Ferris wheel and then we'll get cotton candy."

"Perfect."

Jacob got our tickets. As we waited in line, I pulled the cotton candy off the paper cone, letting it melt in my mouth. I wanted to start over again with everything, my life, all of it. I would never tell Jacob about my past, about Isabel, Belmont, or Sheff. If I was truly going to reinvent myself, I'd have to do more than burn paper and vinyl. I'd have to burn the old Gloria too.

On the Ferris wheel, he sat with his leg pressed to mine. We went up and down, over and under, accordion music coming from the speakers. From high up, the beach looked white, the ocean green, the bathers inconsequential. Jacob inhaled my blonde curls and whispered, "I love you, Gloria Ricci." I felt my body shrink in the metal swing. We rocked back and forth. I took a deep breath. "I love you too." *No shrinking, Gloria. No shirking! You can do this. You can be this woman.* I didn't love him. Of course not, but I was participating, joining the land of the living.

He kissed my neck.

I smiled.

When the Ferris wheel stopped to let riders off, we were at the top, our feet dangling, the crowd shrunken and spotlighted. Jacob took my face in his hands and kissed me. "You make me so happy." *Slide your hand up the back of my neck again. Just do it. And we'll stay like this forever.* He didn't, but I imagined his hand there.

At the bottom, the ride operator swung our door open. "Hope you two lovebirds had fun."

"We did. Thanks." I remembered Turtle Pond. Jacob took my hand, and we started walking toward Mary and Harry's, a one-story motel on Ocean Avenue across the street from the boardwalk. Jacob wrote our names down as Mr. and Mrs. Jacob Blount. I was a little disappointed. It would've been more exciting to put our real names. More scandalous. More seedy. The man behind the desk handed Jacob the key, and we parked in front of room six. Our window faced the parking lot. Jacob closed the curtains, and the passing headlights cast the room in a red light. Everything smelled of mildew. The carpeting was stained and dotted with cigarette burns.

When I climbed into bed, I expected things to be like they'd been, but Jacob said, "I want to make love to you, Gloria. I know you're a virgin, but it's okay because we love each other."

Isabel had put her fingers inside me, but I guessed that I was technically still a virgin. I inched my underwear off, and Jacob spread my legs apart. "It'll hurt less if your legs are spread wide." There was no foreplay. He climbed on top of me and forced himself inside me. "So tight," he said, bearing down. My insides burned. He burrowed his face in my neck as he pushed himself in deeper. Then, he got into a rhythm, his eyes closed, and I tried to relax, to not think, but I did think: *I'm doing this. I can do this. This isn't horrible.* He was moaning. He was covered in sweat, his jaw clenched. As soon as I thought, *When will this be over?* it was over.

Jacob collapsed beside me. "Are you okay?"

"I'm okay." I pulled the sheet up to cover myself.

"It gets better the more you do it. You'll get to where you really like it." I doubted that I would ever *really* like it, but I was going to try. He fell asleep, and I went to the bathroom and showered.

We did it again in the morning. This time, he looked at me. "You just need to relax. Your thighs are like a vise."

"I'm trying."

When it was over, he said, "You're the best thing that's ever happened to me."

"Same here." I went to the bathroom to clean up. When I came out, I said, "I promised my mom that I'd call her this morning. I'm going to find a phone." I slipped on my shoes.

He said, "I love you," before rolling over. Once outside, I walked purposefully toward the ocean. The east wind blew my hair straight back. I'd made a decision. I was going to be with Jacob. *Life isn't perfect. It's never perfect, and it's not possible to live how I'd choose to live, to find a beautiful girl and settle down. It won't happen. It'll never happen. Look what happened to you, darling Sheff. God, I miss you.* I crossed the boardwalk. A flurry of handbills whipped in the wind. They blew across my feet, one of them sticking to my calf. I grabbed it, glancing down. *One Night Only, Madame Zelda, World-Famous Fortune-Teller.* The salty wind struck my face. The waves beat the shore. I folded the handbill and slipped it in my front pocket. Jacob was my fortune.

When I got back to the room, I was out of breath. Jacob said, "Oh no. Was your mother awful?"

"No. Not awful." I took off my clothes and climbed in bed beside him. "I just need to sleep a while longer."

19

CORA BROKE HER ARM THE same week I met Jacob. She couldn't have been happier about falling down a flight of stairs. At the hospital, she met the doctor and potential husband of her dreams. "Let's double-date," she suggested. We were eating lunch in the break room.

"Why not? I'll ask Jacob."

That night, I was staying over at Jacob's. We'd just finished making love when I brought it up.

"Nah. I don't do those."

"What do you mean, 'I don't do those'?"

"Double dates."

"Why not?"

"Too many people. I'm an introvert."

"I think it'll be fun. Cora says that he's a really nice guy."

"I don't like doctors."

"I think he's actually a resident, not a full doctor yet. Come on. He won't be examining you or anything."

"If it'll make you happy . . . I'll go."

Cora and I made arrangements. We planned to see *Dirty Harry* at the drive-in. I packed blankets, and Jacob packed a cooler. My mother said, "Where are you going?"

"To the drive-in."

"You really like this guy?"

"I've been telling you."

She closed my bedroom door and came and sat beside me. "Your dad and I want you to be happy. That's all we've ever wanted."

"That's what I'm doing. I'm being happy." I thought, *I'm being like everybody else. I'm making life easier.*

She hugged me. I rarely noticed her scar from the car accident, but that afternoon, I felt the damaged skin against my cheek. I said, "I love you."

She kissed my forehead. "We love you."

"Gotta go. Dirty Harry is waiting on us." I went out to the front porch to wait for Jacob. When he pulled up, I ran to his truck, tossing my blankets in the back. I was excited. As soon as I opened the door, he said, "I hope this guy isn't a dick."

"Cora likes him."

"Because he's a doctor. I'm just saying, Gloria, that guys who go to medical school tend to think they're smarter than everybody else."

"Just give the guy a chance." I slipped off my shoes and put my bare feet on the dashboard.

When we pulled up to Cora's house, Cora and Richard were sitting on the front stoop. Jacob and I got out of the truck. Cora said, "We get to ride in the back." She introduced Richard to Jacob. Richard said, "And you're the amazing tie girl. Cora told me that you know everything there is to know about men's neckwear, including its history."

"It's true."

"Pleased to make your acquaintance."

"Likewise."

Jacob said, "Jesus. She sells ties," and got in the truck.

In the cab, I said, "He seems nice."

"Because he's sucking up to you. That's how they are."

"Who's they?"

"The doctors and the lawyers."

I didn't say anything.

When we got to the drive-in, Richard insisted on paying. Instead of saying "Thank you," Jacob said, "Fine."

We managed to get a good spot. Cora and I arranged the blankets in the truck bed. Jacob passed out beers from the cooler. Richard tried hard to make small talk with Jacob, but he was being an antisocial jackass. I never should've said yes to the double date. If nothing else, I'd learned that if Jacob didn't want to do something, I should just roll with his decision. When Jacob went to the bathroom, I told Cora, "I'm really sorry that he's being such a jerk."

She whispered, "This is why I want the doctor. He has a good bedside manner."

During the movie, Richard and Cora whispered jokes about *Dirty Harry* while Jacob sat with his feet dangling from the bed, occasionally shushing Richard. "I'm trying to watch the movie."

When I said, "What's going on with you?" he said, "Nothing. I'm fine. What's going on with you?" I gave up.

After we dropped Cora and Richard at her house, Jacob started talking. "That guy was the pits. Cora's an idiot if she keeps dating him."

"I don't get it," I said. "What did he do?"

"Well, for starters, he went on and on about you and your ties. It was patronizing. Then, he had to pay for the drive-in. Of course he did. He was an arrogant dick."

"I thought he was nice." I was eager to get home.

"Do you want to spend the night?"

"Not tonight."

When he pulled into the driveway, he said, "I know that you're your own person, and I know that you take pride in your work, and that's one of the many things I love about you, but I'm your boyfriend. You might want to consider that. You should be defending me, not some doctor you just met, who, by the way, only wants one thing from Cora. He's never going to marry her."

"I wasn't defending anybody."

"Fine."

I slid down from the truck. Then he said, "You hurt my feelings tonight."

"I just wanted to have some fun . . . I'm sorry." I pushed the door closed and went inside. My mother was awake reading one of her textbooks. "How did it go?"

"It was fine. I'm tired."

"Do you want to talk about it? How was the movie?"

"Just tired."

The next morning, Jacob telephoned at seven. Before I could say anything, he said, "I'm sorry about last night. I just felt like you were taking Dr. Dickhead's side."

"There weren't sides."

"But there were. He's going to be some rich doctor, and I work with my hands. I'm a paver and a bricklayer. We're different people, and he thought he was better than me. Anyway, that's on me. I shouldn't have taken it out on you."

I wasn't sure what to say.

"I'm always going to be here for you," he said. "I love you, and I don't want to lose you because of Cora's doctor. I'm sorry for how I acted."

"You're not going to lose me."

"He was just so arrogant."

The next day, I saw Cora at Bink's. She came over to the tie counter. "Jacob is a bad man."

"He's not a bad man."

"You shouldn't defend him."

We never spoke again.

※

A week later, Gwen invited us to dinner. At first, I was understandably hesitant, but Jacob said, "I'm dying to meet her. She's important to you, right?"

"She is."

Jacob drove over, and we walked hand in hand from my house to hers. Jacob said, "She's the one who took you to see *Peter Pan* in the city, right?"

"Right, that's her."

Gwen opened the door. She wore a pink rhinestone clip in her hair and a pink apron. I heard Marlene Dietrich's sultry voice. "Come in. Come in. You're right on time."

Jacob said, "*Blue Angel* is one of my favorite films." I hadn't introduced them, and already Gwen was telling him that her father had met Marlene Dietrich in France during the war. She took Jacob by the arm and led him to her sitting room, where Eugene had his head in a book. She clapped her hands, then nudged Eugene's shoulder.

"Honey, the kids are here."

Eugene closed his book and looked up. "Where?"

"There's Gloria there, and there's her beau. This is Jacob."

Jacob and Eugene shook hands.

"Do you want to make the martinis, or I can do it?" Gwen asked.

Eugene grimaced. "Come on, woman. I'm still handy for a few things." He went to the liquor cabinet.

Gwen said, "Gloria's been keeping you from me."

"It stops now," Jacob said.

Eugene passed out the drinks and sat back in his chair. Gwen asked Jacob about his future plans, and he said, "I want to make a life with Gloria."

I sipped from my martini, then smiled.

"Those are smart plans," Gwen said. I nodded, but after what had happened at the drive-in, I didn't know if I could build a future with Jacob. I didn't think his thinking was in line with mine.

After he'd drunk half of his martini, Eugene asked Gwen to dance. Jacob followed suit. "May I have this dance?"

"Of course."

The way that he slipped his hand up the back of my neck was familiar and never failed to seduce me. I felt his breath in my ear. He said, "I'm crazy about you." The four of us danced in the cramped space. Later, Eugene and Jacob talked about building permits. Eugene said, "It's a racket. I want to build onto my house. It's my house and my land. Why do I need a permit from the county? It drives me bonkers."

Gwen said, "You're already bonkers."

We sat down to a dinner of roast pheasant and creamy

rice. For dessert, Gwen served a chocolate torte. Jacob complimented her cooking. His table manners were impeccable.

When we were getting ready to leave, Gwen put her arm around me and said, "I like him very much."

A week later, Jacob proposed.

I said yes. *I'm living.*

20

THE NIGHT BEFORE THE WEDDING, my father came to my bedroom door. His light eyes were sad. There were wrinkles I hadn't noticed. It frightened me to see him look so old. "You can always come home. You always have a home here. I just want you to know that."

"I know. Thank you."

My mother came in next. "You don't have to do this. It's not too late." She sat on the bed, and I pulled the Bishop book from my nightstand, turning to the fish poem. She took it from my hands, scooting back on the bed. I rested my head in her lap, and she began reading. By the time she got to the end where "everything was rainbow, rainbow, rainbow! And I let the fish go," I was asleep.

Jacob and I got married on Saturday, June 19. We'd known

each other for all of ten weeks. Our ceremony was small. My parents and the Babineauxs were in attendance. The chapel's corridor was lined with matted portraits of priests and bishops, some of whom I recognized.

Father led me to Jacob, who squeezed my hand reassuringly. His dark eyes were glossy, and there was the most beautiful violet light pouring through the stained glass window. I felt a lump in my throat. I was nervous. I hadn't put my trust in another person in a very long time. Then I saw a few honeybees zipping in the light. No one else noticed them. I wiggled my fingers in Jacob's strong hands, feeling that Sheff was there with us. Maybe he'd come with the bees. Come from the other side, as Madame Zelda had said.

The young priest spoke the chosen liturgy. He was a pimply fellow I didn't know. Father O'Connell had adamantly refused to marry me to a non-Catholic. We had no Mass because our union was not a holy sacrament or ecclesiastical union. The diocese had granted us permission to wed only after I agreed to raise my children as Catholic. The church was important to my parents.

Standing there, waiting for the ceremony to be over, I felt lopsided, like my left shoe was too big, like my left leg and left foot had suddenly shrunk. I heard one of the bees buzzing in my ear. Then it felt like my foot and the shoe were gone. I was off balance, dizzy. Then I was falling. Jacob's hands were under my arms. The bee stung behind my ear. My knees brushed the carpet.

As Jacob lifted me up, my mother said, "Are you all right?" The priest, my father, and Gwen asked the same thing. Jacob said, "I'll always catch you." I felt an electric vibration shoot down my neck, the bee sting. My skin was vibrating. I said, "I do," before the priest asked the question. I said it again at the right time. As we stepped down from the dais, I saw the honeybee dead by my foot.

Jacob said, "We did it!"

Outside, his truck was decorated with shaving cream. Oscar was in the truck bed, barking and wagging his tail. There was a cardboard sign tied above the license plate. *Just Married.*

We were driving to Jacob's hometown, to Greeley, North Carolina, so I could meet and celebrate with my in-laws. "Just you wait," he told me. "You're going to love Greeley." We planned to live as purists, or he had plans that we would live as purists, and I'd agreed. Sitting in the truck, my satin gown bunched between my legs, I waved to my family. I still felt the sting from the bee.

"We love you," my mother shouted. Gwen threw rice. Then, we were on our way. I was quiet, pensive, understanding that this was a big step, that I was maybe trying to be someone I wasn't, but I had chosen to be happy. I'd made a choice. As we merged onto the interstate, Oscar settled in the truck bed. "Will he be all right back there?" I asked.

"He's fine. We've traveled a lot."

This is how people live. I'm doing it.

Eighty miles south of Maryville, the radio station fading

and crackling with static, the car full of cigarette smoke, I fell asleep, dreaming bees. I was running through the pines behind my parents' house, and when I got to the creek, the bees enveloped me. I was a vibrating mass of yellow and black noise. I woke in a cold sweat.

Jacob said, "Are you all right?"

I thought of Sheff and his nightmares. "I'm fine."

As the hours passed, I felt uncomfortable in my dress. I kept sliding across the seat. Jacob said, "I'm excited for you to meet Big Mama."

"Who?"

"My mama. We call her Big Mama."

"Oh. I didn't know. And your father and your siblings. It's exciting. I'm an only child."

"Not them."

"What do you mean?"

"My daddy's worthless. You don't want to meet him."

"He'll be at the party."

"He and Big Mama are divorced, and Meredith is in New York, and Clarence and I don't speak." Jacob pushed the lighter in and turned the radio dial. "Clarence is in Africa doing missionary work."

"If your sister's in New York, we should've gone to see her."

"She doesn't want to see me. We had a falling-out. I don't have any use for her."

"You didn't say that your parents were divorced." I took the truck lighter after Jacob and lit a cigarette.

162

"I didn't? I meant to."

I said no more. When we stopped for gas, the fumes made me feel nauseous. Jacob returned from the station with a package of Hostess Cupcakes. "For the bride and groom." I wasn't hungry, but I took a cupcake.

"I don't feel so good," I told him.

"It's probably the heat. We're going to stop in Raleigh and get a good night's sleep before the party tomorrow."

I ate a sliver of icing. It was like eating chocolate-flavored wax. I set the cupcake by my feet and heard Oscar pawing the truck bed. I turned to see him licking the glass. Jacob said, "He really likes you."

"I like him too."

It was after ten o'clock when we stopped at a Motel 6 off I-95 just north of Raleigh. My back and thighs sweating in the slick gown, I was desperate to undress and shower. After getting the key, he said, "We're going to do this right."

"What right?"

"I'm going to carry you over the threshold. We don't want bad luck. But first, let me get Oscar a bowl of water." Jacob took the dog into the motel room and came back for me. He put one arm behind my back and the other under my knees, slick with sweat, and hoisted me up. "I like holding you in my arms."

I smiled as he carried me into the room. It was nice enough, better than Mary and Harry's in Seaside Heights. There was a queen-size bed, two nightstands, two lamps, and one dresser with a small television set on top. Oscar was lying on the foot of the bed. Jacob turned on the TV, kicking off his shoes, while I took a shower. When I came out, he was watching *Marcus Welby, M.D.* "It's not very romantic, is it?"

"It's fine. I'm so tired."

"Aren't you hungry?"

"Actually, I still feel sick. I guess it was the drive."

I got into bed while Jacob went to shower. The TV made the room glow. In no time, I was asleep, only to be awakened by him sliding my nightgown up my legs. He said, "It's bad luck if you don't consummate the marriage on the wedding night." This was my honeymoon night, and I felt nothing but exhausted. He kissed me. Then, he was on top of me. And then he was inside me. "You're so tight," he said. "I love it."

21

THE NEXT MORNING, I TOOK another shower and put on a yellow sundress for our party in Greeley. We drove ninety miles east on Route 264 through Saratoga, Belle Arthur, House, and Washington City. Except for Washington City, the towns were small and squat, with little markets where old men, black and white, congregated beneath rusted awnings. I watched the men mop their brows with handkerchiefs. When we drove into Greeley, the sign said, *Welcome to Greely, population 900*, and just under it in smaller print, *Greeley, founded in 1802*. Just as Jacob had described, the spelling was inconsistent. It was so hot, the pavement gave the illusion of being wet.

Jacob said, "The party's at the fire station." When we pulled into the parking lot, it was nearly full. There were two fire trucks and a few dozen old cars. The party was scheduled for noon. We were fifteen minutes late.

Jacob held the door open for me. Then, he called for Oscar, and the dog jumped from the back of the truck. I tugged to unstick the sundress from my back. I knew that my hair was a mess; the humidity made it unruly. Jacob said, "You look pretty." I didn't feel pretty. Oscar walked at Jacob's side. The building was a brick one-story.

Inside, there was a short hallway and another door. I said, "I'm nervous."

"Don't be. Big Mama's going to love you." When Jacob opened the second door, a big cheer went up. People shouted, "Congratulations!" and "Welcome home!" They clapped and hooted. Big Mama was the first one to greet us. She was really big, her face heavy. She had white, straw-like hair that stopped at her shoulders. Jacob said, "This is Big Mama." I extended my hand, but she pulled me in close, holding on. Then, when she let go, she squeezed my hand. "I'm delighted to meet you."

"Same here."

"I didn't even know Jacob was getting hitched until last week."

"It all happened really fast."

"Isn't she pretty?" Jacob said.

"As a picture."

Then, Big Mama stepped aside so that I could meet everyone who'd come to celebrate our wedding. Person after person introduced themselves. I wouldn't remember any of their names, but everyone seemed friendly. After a while, Big Mama said, "Give the girl some room," and led me to a round table in the center of the fire station. All the other tables were rectangular or square, but each table had a vase of black-eyed Susans as a centerpiece. I said, "I love the flowers."

She said, "They're from my garden. I picked and arranged them myself."

"They're beautiful."

Big Mama saw me looking for Jacob.

"He's over there with his daddy." She pointed, and I saw Jacob on the far side of the room, talking with a waif of a humpbacked man. The old man was stuffing a whole deviled egg into his mouth. Dollops of whipped mayonnaise clung to his unkempt whiskers.

Big Mama said, "That's my ex-husband, Buddy. I didn't invite him to the party because he's known to make a scene, but of course he came anyway, so I've got my eye on him. I'm not going to let him ruin this day for y'all."

"Should I go over there?"

"If I were you, I'd avoid Buddy. Knowing him, he'll make a pass at you, and then he and Jacob will have one more reason to fight, and that's the last thing either one of them needs. They both got tempers."

A few young women came over to our table. One of them, a very tall and bony redhead, her elbows and knees more bulbous than her limbs, introduced herself as Poppy. "I'm Jacob's cousin. My mother, Scarlet, was Big Mama's sister, but then she got the pneumonia when I was just a baby, and she died. I was raised up in the same house as JJ and them."

"JJ?"

"That's what folks call Jacob."

I said, "It doesn't sound like Jacob and his siblings get along."

Poppy said, "That's an understatement. Clarence is born again in Christ's blood, and he thinks Jacob is going straight to hell because he claims to be an atheist and some other stuff."

"That's awful," I said. "And Clarence is in Africa, right?"

"Converting savages," Poppy said, "by bribing them with food. If you believe in Jesus, you can have some bread . . . If you don't, no bread for you . . . That sort of thing. Doesn't seem especially Christian." She snorted.

"What does Meredith do?" I asked.

"She works in Manhattan, an assistant to some broker."

"I only just found out that she lived in New York."

"Yeah, she and JJ don't speak hardly either."

Then, Big Mama chimed in. "It breaks my heart. They don't understand that they're going to need each other one day."

I said, "I'm an only child."

"That's what Jacob said. Must've been lonely growing up," Big Mama said.

"Sometimes."

Then, a young woman with thick brown hair and big green eyes introduced herself. "Hi. I'm Betty." She had a curvy figure. The juxtaposition of her lime-green eyes and brown hair was striking. "I went to high school with JJ." She extended her hand, and I didn't want to let go. I had just gotten married, and I felt physically attracted to this woman. I wasn't going to feel guilty about it. It didn't matter. I'd chosen what I wanted. I wanted to be married and have children.

Big Mama said, "Betty made most of the food here."

"Thank you for doing that," I said.

"It's the least I could do. I love Big Mama. She's like a mother to me."

Big Mama smiled. "Betty owns a restaurant and bakery three doors down."

"It's a living."

Big Mama said, "She's the best cook in town. And modest."

Betty said, "Can I make you a plate?"

"What?" I caught myself staring at her lips. "Sure." I watched her walk to the buffet table in black Nancy Sinatra boots and a green miniskirt, the same green as her eyes. Her blouse was white with flowy yellow-and-lime flower-print sleeves.

I glanced over to see Jacob shaking hands with various men. In ratty T-shirts and faded jeans, they looked like hoodlums. Betty came back to the table with a plate: a ham biscuit, macaroni and cheese, and a slice of chocolate cake. Immediately, I went for the cake. It was like I was craving it. "This is incredible," I said, licking my fingers.

"Thank you." She sat beside me. "Do you know that you've moved to a town where there are only twenty people, give or take one or two, over the age of twelve and under the age of sixty?"

"I didn't. I only knew it was small."

"Crazy small! Where are y'all planning to live?"

"Somewhere nearby, I think. We just got married yesterday."

"There's not a lot in the way of jobs around here. Most people have moved away to be closer to the city."

"Jacob has some ideas. He bought a house. I just don't know where. I haven't seen it."

"Well, I'm glad to hear it because you're clearly older than twelve and younger than sixty."

I laughed.

Big Mama said, "Jacob bought the Priddy house on Priddy Lane. He wired money, and I went to the Western Union, then to the bank. Early Bird helped me."

Betty said, "I know that house."

"I should probably know where I'll be living."

"Oh, you're fine," Betty said. "If you married JJ, you must like living by the seat of your pants."

"Not exactly."

Jacob joined us. Poppy said, "JJ, it's nice to see you."

"Call me Jacob."

"We always call you JJ," Poppy said.

"I'm grown up now."

Poppy said, "Did you see Darlene?"

Jacob said, "She better not be here."

I said, "Who's Darlene?"

Poppy mimed like she was locking her mouth and throwing the key away.

Jacob said, "She's nobody."

I said, "I'm going to use the restroom."

There was only one. While I waited, two men got in line behind me. I heard one of them say, "He told Darlene that he was going to bring back a Yankee bride, and damn if he didn't do it."

The other said, "Do you think he knew that Darlene would show up?"

"Of course he knew."

"Those two are a mess."

I was officially curious about Darlene. Just before it was my turn at the bathroom, I turned to the two men. They were probably in their early thirties. I said, "We haven't met. I'm Gloria Ricci Blount, the Yankee bride."

The men fumbled, managing, "It's nice to meet you," but were otherwise speechless.

When I returned to the table, there was a young woman in cutoff jean shorts and a revealing crocheted top, her midriff exposed, standing beside Poppy. She had dark, stringy hair splayed over her shoulders. She wore heavy makeup and popped her gum—something I'd never do. Poppy said, "Gloria, this is Darlene Hemmy."

"Hello." I pretended that I hadn't heard one thing about her.

"Hey."

Big Mama said, "Darlene, this is Jacob's wife, Gloria."

Then, Jacob came up to the table, grabbing Darlene's elbow. "What are you doing here?"

Darlene said, "I'm just trying to meet your bride. Get off me."

Jacob said, "Please excuse me," and pulled Darlene toward a corner of the fire station hall.

I said, "Was she his girlfriend?"

Betty sipped her wine, pink lipstick on the glass, before answering. "Yup."

When Darlene and Jacob returned, Darlene said, "Good luck to you." She had a heavy southern drawl. Then she walked away.

"Who is she?" I asked Jacob.

"She's nobody."

Then, Buddy, Jacob's father, came over. "I want to get some sugar from my new daughter-in-law."

Big Mama said, "Go away. Nobody wants you here, and stop eating my food. I paid for it."

Betty looked at me and smiled, as if to say, *What have you gotten yourself into?* while Buddy grabbed onto me. "You smell good," he said.

"Thanks." Backing up, I put my hand on Jacob's arm. "Can we talk in private?"

"Sure."

We walked toward the buffet table. As he grabbed a chicken

leg, I said, "I overheard two men talking, and they said that you said that you were going to bring home a Yankee bride."

He shook his head. There was fried chicken grease on his chin. "Do you hear yourself, Gloria? They said that I said that I was going to do whatever . . . It's small-town gossip. I should've warned you. It's out of control. You can't get caught up in it. Poppy is the absolute worst too. She works at the post office, so she knows everybody's business."

"But they were talking about Darlene."

"She's my ex-girlfriend, my very ex-girlfriend, and she wasn't invited. Big Mama didn't invite my daddy either, but he showed up."

"Can we please leave now? I'm ready to go."

"Don't let them ruin everything. The party's just getting started."

"But I'm ready to go."

"Big Mama put this all together."

I felt sick to my stomach, and I felt like I might cry. "Just say good-bye for me." I went out to the truck.

22

As soon as Jacob got in the truck, I said, "You never told me about Darlene." Oscar pawed the cab window.

"Are there things in your life that you haven't told me about?"

I wasn't admitting anything. "Did you honestly tell her that you were going to return from New Jersey with a Yankee wife?"

"Yes," he said, gunning the engine, the tires squealing as he took a right on Main Street. In the rearview mirror, I saw Oscar skid across the cab, landing on his side. "I did, and I was joking." Jacob looked at me, jaw clenched. "I didn't know that I would find you, but when I did find you, I knew you were the one, and I wasn't letting you go. I told you: it was love at first sight."

I sat with my arms folded at my chest.

"I love you. Not her!"

"I just feel really uncomfortable. I don't know anyone here."

"Well, that's why we had the party." He pushed the cigarette lighter in, and I pulled a cigarette from the pack between us. "And you made us leave early, so you really didn't have a chance to meet too many people."

"Your ex-girlfriend was there!"

"I don't want you to be mad at me."

I took a deep breath. "It's just a lot."

"I think everybody has an ex," he said. "She wasn't supposed to be there. She wasn't invited."

"I believe you."

We drove five miles outside town, passing small tobacco and soybean farms. There was a field of grazing cattle and a stretch of dense pines. Then, we took a left on Priddy Lane. Jacob said, "This house belonged to Mrs. Priddy. I got it and the land for a steal. We're going to be self-sufficient." Priddy Lane was a dirt road that led to an old farmhouse. The yard was also dirt. The house appeared to be melting in the sun. White paint hung in sheets. It was a colonial-style home, two stories, a door in the center, windows on either side, and five windows on the second level. Jacob opened the truck door for me while Oscar jumped down from the bed. The porch wasn't in terrible shape. At least, I didn't fall through it. Jacob said, "My man Early Bird, who's gonna help me with the salvage business, got us some furniture. I wasn't gonna bring you home to an empty house." The front door was freshly painted a bright red. Jacob said, "I'm carrying you across the threshold."

"Again?"

"You bet." He picked me up. "I used to come to this house when I was a kid. Mrs. Priddy would decorate for Halloween, and a bunch of us would come over and sit here in front of the fireplace. She'd give us candy apples and popcorn. She told ghost stories. She didn't have any kids of her own."

I got back on my feet. Jacob said, "It's the same as I remember. This is where she'd tell the ghost stories." I followed him into the kitchen. The floor was linoleum, a cream color, strips missing, where the room joined a walk-in pantry. There was a single lightbulb and a string to pull the light on. I pulled the string. Two honeybees hovered on the pantry shelf. *Sheff is with the bees.* That's how it felt. That's what I needed to believe.

There was an exterior door off the kitchen that led to a brick patio overgrown with Bermuda grass and weeds. Past the patio, ivy climbed a dead tree. Oscar bounded past me and lifted his leg on the ivy. Then, he ran back indoors. I pulled the door shut.

In the center of the house, the stairs led up to a main hallway with a bathroom and two small bedrooms to the right and a larger bedroom to the left. The floors were oak, in desperate need of refinishing. The doorknobs were crystal. Each door had a skeleton-key lock. I'd always liked skeleton-key locks. They were reminiscent of English novels. The master bedroom had been somewhat restored. The many layers of wallpaper had been stripped down, a fresh coat of white paint applied. There was a tall bed, mahogany, and a matching chest of drawers. I opened one of them, and it smelled of mothballs. Jacob said, "This was Mrs. Priddy's furniture, but the mattress is new." In the middle drawer, I discovered a lavender sachet and put it to my nose. It still smelled. I set it on top of the dresser and opened the one window in the room. Lead dust fell to the sill. The window's glass was thick and wavy. A light breeze blew into the room before I let the window close. I turned to look at Jacob.

"What do you think?" he asked.

"It's nice." The bed was made. "It's really different from the suburbs."

"It's country."

"I think I like country."

I followed him downstairs to the kitchen. There was a refrigerator with a metal handle. Jacob opened it and got a beer. "Want one?"

"You bet."

"Want two?"

"Why not?" Then I laughed, handing him back the second beer. There was a small round kitchen table.

"I'm glad you like it here."

"I really do.

"And we've got four acres."

We sat at the table, drinking our beers. Jacob said, "Here's to Mrs. Blount. I love the way that sounds."

"And to Mr. Blount." We clinked our cans. "Do you want me to start calling you JJ?"

"I'd prefer if you didn't."

"Same here."

We went to bed early. I pulled the covers up to my neck. He kissed me and then rolled over. I stared at the ceiling until exhaustion took over and I slept.

There was a lot to do that first year and very little money. To get on our feet, Jacob went to work on Saturdays and Sundays selling used vinyl, furniture, and estate-sale jewelry at the flea market in Washington City. This was the beginning of the salvage business, the goal of self-sufficiency and purism. I went to work sanding the interior floors while Jacob and his pal Early Bird worked on the exterior, patching and sanding the old wood. Early Bird was a nice fellow. He had maybe eight teeth and bad acne scars, and he spoke in a thick country accent, like nothing I'd ever heard. But he was kind. He always complimented me, even when I was wearing nothing more than a pair of jeans and a T-shirt. He said that Jacob was lucky to have found me.

Summers in Greeley were scorchers. We didn't have an air conditioner, so I spent a lot of time in tank tops and shorts standing in front of the fan, taking cold showers, and drinking ice water. I'd never been so uncomfortably hot. The sun set at nine o'clock and the lightning bugs performed a flickering dance across the grass. Shortly after we'd moved in, I found Mrs. Priddy's turntable and some old records—Bessie Smith, Louis Armstrong, Benny Goodman, and Ella Fitzgerald. Every morning the humidity rose up from the ivy, clover, and dirt with the sun. I understood the meaning of *dog days*. I wore a cap pulled low down to keep the sun off my face. I sprayed Oscar and myself with the hose between digging the weeds out of the brick patio. A hundred feet behind the house, there was a shed filled with rakes, a hoe, a shovel, flowerpots, and a trowel, all left behind after Mrs. Priddy died. I was cleaning it up, knocking down cobwebs, wiping off shelves. I found gardening gloves and imagined the woman who'd worn them, the woman Jacob had spoken of, someone who'd loved children but who'd lived alone, a widow, no babies. Oscar joined me in the shed, the bees trailing us. Oscar ate one and yelped when it stung his tongue. I was worried that he might have a bad reaction, but it was only a minor discomfort as it didn't deter his attempts to eat more. If I shut the shed door, the bees flew into it. I'd hear them butt against the wood, so when I was inside, I left the door open. They gathered over the tool bench and along the ceiling. They flew from one corner to the next, and I would often watch them, thinking about Sheff. Dr. Belmont had liked to keep all the doors shut. The bees liked them open.

Big Mama came for dinner every Sunday. She was on disability due to a bad hip, but for twenty years, she'd worked the cash register at the Greeley Pharmacy. When we all got together, she told the best stories about pharmacy drug thefts and attempted murder by poison. If Poppy happened to come with her, we heard a mound of gossip. She told us who was cheating, who had an illegitimate child, who was getting brown-papered copies of *Playboy* magazine delivered to their post office box. I thought she had to be illegally opening people's mail. On Sundays, we ate well: baked chicken, roast turkey, sometimes steak. Jacob cooked.

During the week, we ate peanut butter sandwiches, canned chili, and SpaghettiOs. Jacob joked that he should've made sure I knew how to cook before he married me. I thought I was doing just fine. I could steam vegetables in the colander, scramble eggs, make a box of macaroni and cheese, and boil spaghetti. Good enough.

In August, we got a telephone. I was elated. I'd been writing letters back and forth with my parents and Gwen. I could finally talk to them. It'd been nearly two months since I'd seen or spoken to anyone from Maryville. Then Jacob said, "No long-distance phone calls. We can't afford it."

"What about on Sundays? The rate is lower on Sundays."

"Once a month on Sundays."

I decided that that first Sunday in August would be my first once-a-month. I called my parents at two o'clock when I knew they'd be home from Mass. The first thing I said was, "I have a telephone!"

My father said, "It's good to hear your voice. How's married life?"

Jacob was at the flea market with Early Bird. "Good. Different."

"We miss you," he said. "We worry about you."

"Jacob's mother has been amazing, and his cousin Poppy is quite the character."

He said, "I'm glad to hear it. Have you found a job?" He knew how much I'd enjoyed my job at Bink's.

"I'm working at home," I said. "Remember the purist thing, Dad. We're planning to do everything ourselves. Eventually, we're going to grow our own food and start a salvage business. Jacob says that it's wasteful to want everything brand-new. The best appliances were made ten or twenty years ago."

My dad said, "Um, okay." He obviously didn't agree. "Your mother's about to rip the phone out of my hand. Let me pass you over to her."

"Hi, sweetheart. It's been so good to get your letters. We miss you terribly."

"I miss you too."

"Are you coming home for Christmas?"

Jacob had already said that we couldn't afford such extravagances, adding, "We have our own home. Why am I going to sleep under another man's roof?"

"No. Not this year."

"We can pay for your gas."

"Jacob wants to have our first Christmas in our own home."

"What do you want?"

"Mother . . . He's my husband."

"I have some news."

"What is it?" I was glad she'd changed the subject.

"I've transferred to a four-year college."

"That's wonderful."

"Right now, I'm taking a class in western literature and another called Women's Studies. It's fascinating."

I wished that I could reach out and hold her, take her hand in mine. We'd come full circle, us girls, mother and daughter. We'd both mourned. We'd both survived.

She said, "If you ever want to talk, you call collect. Do you understand me?"

"I do, Mother."

"And we'll mail your Christmas presents. We love you so much."

When I hung up, I stared at the phone, sadder than before I'd called. Hearing their voices had only made me miss them more.

23

IN NOVEMBER, THE BEES DISAPPEARED. Jacob worked with Early Bird every day except Mondays. The weekends were their busiest days because the flea markets were open Fridays, Saturdays, and Sundays. Jacob started traveling to estate sales, buying furniture and appliances he thought he could fix up and sell for a profit.

Gwen and my parents phoned at least every other day. Jacob didn't mind—so long as we weren't paying for it.

The first week in December, Betty Jenkins telephoned the house. "Hi," she said, "this is Betty. We met at your fire station wedding party."

"How could I forget that extravaganza?"

"Seriously. I bet you really loved the ex-girlfriend part."

"I never saw that coming. Who does that?" I laughed.

Betty said, "Darlene Hemmy, that's who. Listen, I was wondering if you were up for some company? I need to run a few errands, and I thought I'd swing by, visit, check out your house. Rumor has it that you've made a lot of repairs."

I hadn't seen her in nearly five months. "Sure. That would be nice." I was allowed to have friends. Just because I'd been attracted to her at the fire station all those months ago didn't mean that I'd feel anything now. Beside I'd never act on such feelings.

"Terrific. I'll see you in about an hour."

I jumped in the shower. I was outside throwing a tennis ball to Oscar when she pulled up in a Volkswagen convertible, the top down. Her hair was tied back in a blue ribbon.

She got out of the car. "I love this dog." Oscar ran to her, dropping his ball at her feet. She threw it for him. "I used to play sports. Now I bake, and it shows." She bent over and pulled a red tin, a shiny silver bag, and a bottle of wine from her back seat. "I brought a very belated housewarming present."

"You didn't have to do that."

"Thanks for letting me come over. I didn't know how long the honeymoon stage lasted, but I talked to Big Mama, and she said that you'd appreciate some company."

"She was right. Come on in."

Betty said, "I haven't been in this house since I was a little girl."

"At Halloween?"

"Exactly."

"Jacob has the same memories." Then, I said, "I love your

outfit." She wore a blue floral shirt with flowy sleeves and faded bell-bottoms.

"Any excuse to dress up, and I'm all over it. I spend most days in an apron, flour in my hair and everywhere else. Oh, here." She handed me the red tin, the wine, and the little bag. "Do you like coconut and walnuts?"

"I sure do."

Betty followed me to the kitchen. I peeked inside the tin. "Oh, have one," she said. "They're chocolate chip, coconut, and walnut, because you can never have too much goodness in one cookie."

I bit into one. "So good! Big Mama brings your desserts sometimes when she comes to Sunday dinner."

Betty laughed. "I love that woman. She keeps me in business."

I set the cookies and wine on the counter.

"Open the present. It's just a little something."

I pulled out the tissue paper. Then, the gift.

"They're tea towels," she said. "I got them at the Biltmore Estate in Asheville. I thought they were so cute."

"I love them." I had some raggedy secondhand dish towels from the thrift store. I pulled them from the oven railing, replacing them with Betty's.

"I'm glad. Now, let's have a glass of wine and celebrate your house and your marriage and no ex-girlfriends lurking about."

"I'll drink to that." I looked for a corkscrew. I opened one drawer. Then another. Then, a third. "All we drink is beer."

She pulled one from her purse, uncorking the bottle. "I own a restaurant." I poured us each a glass. Then, I gave her a tour. She said, "You should come shopping with me."

"I don't really shop."

"That's why Jacob married you." Betty followed me to our living room. "But seriously, you'll have to day-trip to Raleigh with me. I am the queen of bargain shopping, and I'm a bit of a clothes whore, but around here, nobody dresses up. So I dress up and go shopping."

"Maybe."

"It's nearly Christmas. You celebrate Christmas, right? So you'll want to buy a present or two."

Betty sat on the sofa. It was a hideous upholstered green-and-orange basket-weave print that Jacob had found. I sat Indian-style on our rug. I said, "It's snowing at my parents' house. Snow makes me think of Christmas, not this sixty-plus-degree weather."

"So you miss it?" she asked.

"More than I thought I would."

"Sometimes we get ice in Greeley, but never snow. My uncle Aubrey lives in Colorado, and before my mom got sick, we went to see him. There was so much snow there, and mountains. It was beautiful, and I remember feeling like I'd just stepped through the wardrobe into Narnia."

"I love those books."

Betty said, "I was an English major in college."

"Really? I love to read."

"I graduated from UNC–Chapel Hill in 1966. I was going to live in Durham, but then my mama got sick. I came home and ended up opening a bakery. It grew into a restaurant, just breakfast and lunch, but it's good. One day, I'd like to write a cookbook."

"That's really impressive."

"Not so much, not really. Greeley is most certainly not where I thought I'd be at twenty-seven years old. I was getting out of Greeley and never looking back."

I got up and put on my new album, *Tapestry* by Carole King, a gift from Gwen. Betty said, "How's married life?"

"Really good. Working hard."

"The house looks good. Big Mama said that y'all painted the exterior yourself."

"Mostly Jacob and Early Bird. I did the floors."

"Well, it looks great. Mrs. Priddy would be proud. It's awful to see a home fall into ruin."

Betty knew the words to every Carole King song. *You just call out my name, and you know wherever I am, I'll come running to see you again.* Betty's full lips were stained burgundy. "I hope you haven't heard any more from Darlene."

"No. Thank God."

"She and Jacob were that on-again, off-again couple. They fought constantly. After high school, they moved in together. One of them was always pissing the other one off, and everybody who knew them took sides. It was like the Hatfields and the McCoys."

"Whose side did you pick?"

"I went to college. I got the hell out of here. When I came back, I couldn't believe that the same drama I remembered from high school was still going on. It's kind of depressing."

I confided in Betty: "He apparently told Darlene that he was going to come home with a Yankee wife."

"I heard all about that at the restaurant. Gossip. I wouldn't give one hoot about it."

"You're right. It was just so weird. Rather unsettling."

"I'm here if you need a sympathetic ear. Small-town living is not easy like you'd think. Everybody is always up in your business."

"Thanks." I asked Betty, "Are you married?"

"Not in the cards. I live alone, and I like it that way."

I went to the kitchen for the bottle of wine and the cookie tin. "Do your parents live in Greeley?"

"My dad passed away ten years ago, and my mom lives in a nursing home. When I came back after graduation to visit, she was really confused. She forgot my dad's name. Then, when she remembered that she'd forgotten it, she became very upset. She kept forgetting things. It seemed to get worse in a matter of weeks. She kept saying, 'I can't lose my mind. Don't let me forget everything.' It's been a tough five years." Betty made a weird noise like she was stifling a sneeze. Then, I saw that she was tearing up. "I don't like to cry," she said, "but it's really hard sometimes. My mom has good days and bad days. More bad than good."

"I'm sorry."

"I wouldn't be in Greeley except I need to be here. My mom used to live with me, up until six months ago when she started wandering off. When I'd find her, she wouldn't know me. I'd try to take her home, and she'd fight me."

"That's awful. I'm so sorry."

"She's only fifty-nine. I never thought of her as old. I look just like her."

I didn't know what to say. I poured the last of the wine into her glass.

"And I wonder why I have no friends? Jesus, but I'm depressing."

"No, you're not."

I saw Jacob's truck pulling into the driveway. He came in through the kitchen, and I went to meet him. I reached out my hands to tell him that I was having a great time with Betty when he said, "What is she doing here?"

"She brought us cookies and tea towels."

"Have you been drinking?"

"Just a little wine."

"During the day?"

"It's after five. What does it matter?"

Then, Betty came into the kitchen. "I should go. It's already dark. I had fun, Gloria."

"Me too."

Jacob got a beer from the refrigerator. "See ya."

I walked Betty out to her car. We hugged. She smelled like the cookies she'd brought. "You're a fun one," she said.

"Back at you." As she drove away, I waved. Her dark ponytail caught the wind. I was angry that Jacob had said, "What is
she doing here?" When I went back inside, he was sitting at the
kitchen table, drinking his beer and eating the cookies she'd
brought. I said, "Why were you so rude?"

"I wasn't rude. I said, 'See ya.' I'm not a big fan. She went
away to school, and she should've stayed away. She thinks she's
better than everybody else."

"I don't think so."

"You just met her. Big Mama goes to her bakery all the
time. That's her excuse for hanging around her. What's yours?"

"You're being mean. Her mother was sick."

"I don't know her mother."

I started washing our wineglasses, and Jacob came up behind me. He kissed my neck. "I missed you today." I was thinking about Betty, about her wine-stained lips. Jacob slipped his
hands between my waist and the sink. He started unbuttoning
my shirt. I pretended his hands were Betty's. He said, "We
own this house. Let's do it right here on the kitchen floor." His
mouth belonged to Betty.

We got down on the cracked linoleum.

"I missed you today."

I straddled him, my eyes closed. He was Betty. For a second, I worried that I was cheating, thinking of Betty, but then
I decided I didn't care.

24

I TOOK PRIDE IN MY work. I painted our bedroom a bright yellow. I collected enough Green Stamps to surprise Jacob with a television for Christmas. I planted grass seed in the fall, and it came up in the spring. I got rid of the weeds overtaking the brick patio. Jacob collected old pieces of picket fencing at the flea market, and he and I were slowly putting a whole fence together around our house. I felt like I was really succeeding, living that American dream—even the picket fence.

On March 26, three days before my twenty-third birthday, my mother called from a hotel in Washington City. They'd flown into Raleigh and rented a car. "Surprise," she said, and then before I could say anything, she said, "We didn't see you at Thanksgiving or for Christmas, and I told you that your father and I would come to you, but you said, 'No, we want our first Christmas to be just the two of us together,' and your father and I were okay with that, sweetheart, but we haven't seen you now in nine months. We miss you. So we're in town, or at least close to Greeley. We found an okay place, and we don't have to see you every day, but we don't want to miss your birthday, and we could see you for Easter too if that would be all right. If they have Catholic churches down here, we could go to Mass."

I tried to speak, but she cut me off. "I hope you aren't mad. You're our only daughter. We love you." She stopped.

"I'm thrilled. I'll talk to Jacob and see what he's planned for my birthday, and I'll call you back. I think there's a Catholic church in Washington City, but I know there isn't one in Greeley."

"Okay," my mother said. "We'll be here."

I hung up the phone.

When Jacob got home from work, I got him a beer and opened it. Then, I sat on his lap. "So, guess what?"

"I have no idea."

I smiled exaggeratedly. "My parents are in Washington City!"

He swigged his beer. "Why?"

"They miss me."

"You're a grown woman. Why can't they let you live your own life?"

"They miss me." I smiled again, trying to look cute.

"Get off," he said.

I stood up, and he lit a cigarette. "What do you need me to do?"

"I don't need you to do anything. It's my birthday on Wednesday and Easter is Sunday, and since they didn't see me at Christmas, they flew down to surprise me."

"Surprise? I think it's inconsiderate."

"Why?"

"It just is."

"I'm their only child."

"I guess if they have that kind of money to throw away flying up and down the East Coast, so be it."

"Please don't be disagreeable."

He got another beer from the fridge. "I'm going to take a shower. When are they coming over?"

"I was hoping we could invite them over tonight. If that's all right. I didn't want to make any plans until I checked with you. I told my mother that I'd call her back."

"It doesn't really matter what I think." He tromped upstairs. I waited until I heard the bathroom door open and close before I picked up the telephone.

Then I heard the bees buzzing, and pulled back the pantry curtain. There was a tiny hole where the left corner of the pantry ceiling connected to the exterior wall and then to the wood siding. I hung the phone up and went into the pantry. With the light off, I could see the pink twilight through the crevice, and I could see the worker bees constructing cells. I watched the bees work. After a while, I slid the curtain closed and telephoned my mother at her hotel. "Do you want to come over around seven?"

"Absolutely!"

I heard my dad in the background. "Tell her that we'll bring some cheese and crackers. Tell Jacob that I can make him a gin fizz."

"Tell Dad that we don't have any gin. If he wants, he can pick up some beer."

"We'll do it," my mother said. "We'll see you in an hour."

"Okay." I hung up.

I went upstairs and opened the bathroom door. Jacob was stepping out of the tub. I said, "Please don't be in a bad mood. Please don't be angry that they're in town."

He grabbed a towel off the rack. "It's fine." He didn't say anything else.

I went downstairs to see what we had in the way of food. Lots of canned chili and ravioli, some Hostess Sno Balls and Fritos, but little else. I was closing the pantry curtain when Jacob came downstairs, his hair slicked back. He kissed me. "I'm sorry about earlier. It's just rude to visit someone without asking. I feel like we're not prepared. I'm going to run out and get some beer and some crackers."

"I think my dad's bringing beer. He said he'd bring some cheese and crackers."

"I'll grab something else then," he said.

"I'm sorry that they didn't tell us they were coming."

"Don't be sorry. Like you said, you're their only daughter. I was just being a dick."

"Should I call your mom?" I asked. "They'll want to meet her."

"Whatever you want to do."

My parents arrived promptly at seven o'clock. Oscar barked like crazy when their rental car pulled into the driveway. He ran ahead of me, nearly knocking me over. Jacob caught up with us, taking hold of my hand. My mother's arms were outstretched. "Your house is lovely," she said.

"Thank you."

Jacob and my father shook hands. Jacob said, "We're so glad you're here. What a great surprise."

My father said, "Gloria's been telling us about her home-improvement skills. I had to see it to believe it."

Jacob said, "She can't cook, so I figured she had to be good at something."

"Ha-ha," I said.

My mother chimed in. "She got a C in home economics."

"That's enough out of you two," I said.

My dad pulled a twelve-pack of beer, a box of Ritz Crackers, and a block of cheddar cheese from the trunk. Jacob offered to help, and my dad handed him the twelve-pack. My parents followed us and Oscar indoors. Together, Jacob and I took them on a tour of the house. Jacob highlighted all the home-improvement things I'd done. "She painted in here," he said. "She sanded these floors." When we got to the bathroom, he said, "We still need to redo the tile. You can see where it's cracked in spots. Gloria scraped all the loose bits already so it's safe to walk in here and everything. Plus," he said, swigging his beer, "eventually we'll have to retile that wall. We can do it all at once."

My father said, "I'm really impressed by both of you. I couldn't have done all this."

"Thanks, Dad."

"I mean it."

We went back downstairs. My mother said, "The kitchen is small."

"It's just the two of us."

She looked in the pantry. "What's that noise?"

"Nothing." I pulled the curtain shut.

We went and sat in the living room. My father liked blues and jazz, so I put on Mrs. Priddy's Bessie Smith record. I sat on the floor so my parents could sit on the sofa. Jacob sat in his recliner. "When was the house built?" my father asked.

"Nineteen twenty-seven," Jacob said. "A tobacco farmer named Aster Priddy built it. He and his wife, Marla, lived here with their daughter, Beatrice, and Beatrice lived here until she died."

My mother and I went to the kitchen for beers. She said, "School's going well."

"My friend Betty graduated with a bachelor's degree in English from the University of North Carolina."

"Maybe I can meet her."

"Well, if you want anything decent to eat while you're in town, you'll have to meet her. Betty has a bakery and restaurant. And you know me: I can't cook."

"I think you told me about Betty."

"She's really nice . . . Is Uncle Eddie still in town?" I poured Fritos into a bowl.

Mother said, "They can wait on those beers." We sat at the kitchen table, popping open two of the beers. "So your uncle has moved to Miami. He's written to tell us that he's in love with someone named Honey. She's Cuban, one of those refugees."

"Wow! I guess that's a good thing—as long as he's happy."

"I don't think that man will ever be happy."

"You seem happy."

"I am. This semester I'm taking an Afro Studies course. It's so interesting, and I'm on spring break like a real college kid." She laughed. "It took long enough."

"How's Dad doing with his hand?"

"Better all the time, really. He has some arthritis, they think. He had an X-ray taken, but considering how many bones he broke, he's doing better than anyone anticipated."

"How's Gwen?"

"You probably know better than I do. I bet she calls you every day."

"Actually, she does."

We both laughed.

My mother said, "Are you happy? We were so upset that we didn't see you at Christmas."

"I'm good. We should take these to Jacob and Father."

She patted my hand. "Are you sure you're all right? You didn't know Jacob for very long before you married him."

"We're really good."

"Okay." She knew that I wanted her to stop prying. She followed me to the den. I handed a beer to my father and one to Jacob. Bessie Smith lamented, *Nobody knows you when you're down and out.*

I said, "Mrs. Priddy left her phonograph and records."

"Great record collection," my father said.

Jacob said, "We should have a cookout for your birthday, Gloria. That way, your parents can meet Big Mama and Early Bird."

"And Poppy . . . and Betty."

I hadn't kept my distance from Betty. In fact, in February, I had walked three miles to town, to her restaurant. I sat at the red Formica-topped bar and ordered a bowl of tomato bisque and a slice of blueberry pie, the whole time hoping and wishing that she'd come out from the kitchen. I kept looking around for her, eating slowly. I drank three cups of coffee. After I'd finished my pie and my last cup of joe, when I was about to pay the check, she emerged from the back. "What are you doing here? You should've told someone to get me," she said.

"I figured you were busy. Besides, you must know everybody in town."

"Everybody's not as fun as you." She wiped her hands down the front of her apron. "It's great to see you. How have you been?"

We sat and talked for over an hour. The restaurant closed, and she drove me home.

While Jacob talked about my upcoming birthday cookout, I was thinking about Betty. "I'll hire Betty to make a cake."

My mother said, "We can make your cake, Gloria. We can make it together."

"Oh, Mother, no offense, but nobody bakes like Betty."

"Enough said."

My parents stayed until nearly ten o'clock. It was hard saying good-bye. As we stood in the driveway, I thought I might cry. My mother saw it in my face. She hugged me. "We'll see you tomorrow. You can show us around town. Just call when you wake up. We have all week." She kissed my cheek.

The next day, I telephoned my parents early. They came in their rental car to pick me up. There wasn't much to see in Greeley, but I pointed out the Big-T Hamburger joint; Woodrowe's Bar, where Jacob sometimes went with Early Bird; the fire station; the library; and the grocery store. Then, we went to Betty's restaurant for lunch. Betty came out and shook hands with my father. She embraced my mother. "I love your daughter."

My mother whispered to me, "Your friend's very bubbly."

Betty heard her. "They call me Betty Bubbles." She smiled and hugged my mother again. "Better get back in the kitchen."

After we finished our meal, our waitress told us, "Lunch is on Betty."

"Isn't she nice?" my father said.

"She really is."

The next day, my parents took me shopping in Washington City. They bought me a set of dishes and some new pots and pans. I told them that I didn't need them, but they insisted. Later that night, Jacob said, "After your parents are gone, I'll take all that stuff back to the store. We don't need your parents' charity."

I said, "They're just being nice."

"There's nothing wrong with what we have already."

I wasn't going to argue with him.

On my birthday, Big Mama came over early. She brought coleslaw and potato salad. Early Bird pulled up in a borrowed truck with a borrowed gas grill. He had a cooler packed with steaks. He and Jacob set up the grill and four tables they'd borrowed from the fire station. Around four, Betty arrived. She came into the kitchen, carrying a cake box.

"My gift," she said, untying the string and opening the box. It was a three-layer chocolate cake topped with toasted coconut. "Happy Birthday, Gloria." She hugged me. "And I'm taking you shopping. And you're going to like it."

"I want to pay for the cake."

"It's my gift, as is our future shopping trip. I insist."

"It's the most beautiful cake I've ever seen."

"Yay!" She clapped. She was wearing her faded bell-bottoms

and a yellow shirt with cap sleeves. Along the hem were little green flowers. Betty was the only person I knew who looked really good in yellow. I often caught myself staring at her.

Early Bird rushed into the kitchen. "I nearly forgot," he said. "I got these expired potato chips for free." He handed me two bags. "They're only expired by three days, so no one's gonna know the difference." Then, he said, "Happy birthday." The screen door clacked behind him.

"Thanks!" I called.

Betty burst out laughing. "He's a hoot."

My parents arrived at five, and I introduced them to Big Mama and Early Bird. My mother said to Big Mama, "I've heard so much about you. Thank you for taking care of Gloria."

"Oh, she takes care of us. I'm so pleased that she and Jacob found each other."

My father helped Jacob at the grill. I had no idea where Jacob got the money for so many steaks. They weren't skirt steaks either. They were nice cuts of meat. My mother and Betty were talking about their favorite books. Big Mama was shooing flies away from her coleslaw. Then, Jacob told the story of how we first met, how for him it was love at first sight. He said, "I couldn't understand why she was selling nooses, and that's exactly what I said to her, and she still agreed to go out with me. Then, after our first date, I couldn't stop thinking about her. I wanted to be with her every day." He looked at me and raised his beer. "And I was. I love you, honey."

"I love you too."

Everyone was seated when Poppy arrived. She kissed my cheek and apologized for being late. Then, she fixed a plate and found a seat beside Big Mama. My parents were discussing our plans for the next day. Betty was telling Early Bird that she used buttermilk in the chocolate-cake recipe. I heard Poppy whisper to Big Mama, "Millie who works at the Woolworth's saw Jacob's truck at Darlene's house yesterday."

Big Mama smiled at me before saying, "Gloria's not deaf, Poppy." To me, she said, "Don't pay attention to hearsay."

My father's attention had turned to Early Bird and my mother was talking to Jacob. All I wanted to do was get Betty alone and explain, *I'm not sure how I got here. I don't think this is how my life is supposed to be,* but I stirred the coleslaw on my plate, stabbed at my steak, and smiled at Big Mama. "Just gossip," I said. I'd feed my steak to Oscar later. *The thing is, if you get very depressed about something, it's hard as hell to swallow.*

25

It was a sunny spring day. Betty and I and were driving east toward Greeley after a day of shopping in Raleigh when I told Betty what Poppy had overheard. "His truck was at Darlene's house."

"I know where Darlene lives," she said.

"He'd never cheat on me."

"Do you want to drive by there?"

"I don't know." I felt sick to my stomach. I hadn't even been married a year. Why would Jacob be with his ex? Why did I care? I reasoned that it was because I was trying hard to do this American-dream thing, to get it right.

Betty drove into Greeley, taking a left on Wistar Lane. She pointed out Darlene's house. "It's up there, that cinder block one." Betty slowed down. "Oh, shit," she said.

Michele Young-Stone

Jacob's truck was in plain view. "Oh, shit," I echoed.

Betty drove to the end of the street, slowing down, and pulling the parking brake. "What do you want to do, Gloria?"

"I don't know. What should I do?"

"I don't know."

"I could knock on the door."

"You could," Betty said.

"But I don't think I want to do that."

"I don't think I would either."

"Shit," I said.

"Shit," she repeated. "This looks bad."

"Let's just get out of here."

"Are you sure?"

"I'm sure."

"What are you going to do?" We drove toward my house.

"I'm not going to assume the worst. I'm just going to ask him. I'm sure there's some reasonable explanation."

"I bet you're right."

When Betty dropped me off, she said, "Good luck."

Inside, I changed into the new blue sundress she'd bought me in Raleigh. It was sleeveless, fitted at the top with a full bottom that flared when I spun. Betty had also given me a couple bottles of red wine from her restaurant. "They're not selling," she'd said. I was twirling in the kitchen in my new dress when Jacob pulled into the driveway at six o'clock. When he came in through the kitchen door, I said, "How was your day?" *Were you at Darlene's house?*

206

"Not bad. How was yours?" He opened the refrigerator, looking for a beer. There was one left. "I thought you were going to the grocery store."

"No. I went clothes shopping in Raleigh with Betty."

"I don't have any beer."

"There's some red wine on the counter."

"I don't drink wine." He pulled the chair out from under the table, swung it around, and straddled it. "What's for dinner?"

"You drank Chianti with me in Maryville."

"That was different. What's for dinner?" he asked again.

"I don't know. Why am I in charge?"

"Are you serious, Gloria? Have you lost your fucking mind?"

"No."

"Then, you should've planned something for dinner."

I went into the pantry. "I can make spaghetti."

"I'm sick of spaghetti."

I looked to the corner. Through the crevice, I could see the bees circling their hive. I looked back at Jacob sitting at the table. "I saw your truck at Darlene's house."

"What did you say?"

I stepped out of the pantry, my hands behind my back, like I was a kid awaiting a parental verdict. "I saw your truck at Darlene's house."

"No, you didn't."

"Betty and I passed by her house after we went shopping."

He got up, and the chair fell over. "What were you doing on Darlene's street?" His jaw was clenched.

"Poppy saw your truck there." I swallowed, then squeezed my bottom lip.

"Are you spying on me?"

"So, you were there?"

"No. I wasn't there."

"Your truck was there."

"Early Bird borrowed my truck."

"Why?" I put my hands on my hips.

"Something is seriously wrong with you. You're touched in the head. Mental!" With his left hand, he shoved me. Then, he turned, picking up the chair where he'd just sat, throwing it at the cabinets. I covered my ears. One of the legs splintered in two. I backed up, flattened myself against the refrigerator. He passed by, his hands in fists, slamming the door shut as he left. I heard the truck engine start. Oscar came bounding down the stairs.

An hour later, Early Bird was at the kitchen door.

"Hey, Gloria. Can I come in?"

I opened up.

"Listen, Jacob phoned me about a half hour ago. I came over to tell you that he wasn't at Darlene's. He let me borrow his truck because I'm helping her move. My truck bed is all greasy, so we've been swapping sometimes."

"Where is she moving?"

"Washington City."

Early Bird checked the refrigerator for a beer and sat down empty-handed. "He said that you were spying on him and that you don't trust him . . . Maybe you didn't give him a chance to explain. I don't know. I'm no mind reader."

"I don't know either." I poured a glass of wine and sat at the table. Pieces of the broken chair littered the floor.

"He's got a temper," Early Bird said, "but he loves you."

I nodded.

"And he don't love Darlene."

"Why are you helping her?" I asked.

"She's nice enough. She asked." Early Bird shrugged.

"Do you want a glass of wine?"

"I best skedaddle."

I wondered if Jacob was coming home. I stayed up until the late-night news went off, and then I went upstairs to bed. I was a real shit wife, and I knew it. Maybe deep down, I wanted to think he was cheating. It would give me a reason to leave.

The next morning, I woke at six as Jacob was just getting out of bed, pulling on his jeans. "What time did you come home?"

"Late."

"I'm sorry," I said, "for thinking you were with Darlene."

He shook his head disappointedly. "I thought you knew me."

"I do."

"No, you don't." He pulled a T-shirt over his head. "I'm

sorry I pushed you, but you shouldn't have brought up Darlene. I was upset. I told you to leave her and me and all of that alone. It's past history. I don't care about her."

"I won't bring her up again."

One afternoon, I went to the shed for a trowel. I was going to weed the garden. The honeybees trailed, flying through the doorway, swarming the ceiling. I grabbed the gardening gloves and looked up. More came. And more. There were thousands of them. I was astonished. "Is Sheff with you?" I asked, expecting an answer, as odd as that sounds. I watched and waited. They gathered in a T-shaped mass that framed the rafters, and I got down on my knees. Then, down on my back, the gardening gloves still in hand, I waited for them to say something. Rather, they came together, a gold-and-amber disco ball, bees zipping out from the spinning center, then descending, not falling, but aiming, a thousand bullets, on my skin. They were going to kill me maybe, finish what they started when I was seven, but then I felt their tiny fuzzy legs on my skin. My limbs vibrating with theirs. I slipped off my sneakers as the bees crowded onto my face and neck. I was not afraid. We hummed together. Their legs were sticky on my eyelids. Ascending. Defying gravity. They felt like salvation. The sound had walls, tissue thin, and deep inside the cell, I saw Sheff shooting his arm into the air, a rocket, the

bees flying out. We had our whole lives ahead of us. He straddled my red suitcase at the New York Public Library. I shot
my arm into the air. Then, saw that it was golden with bees.
I heard a man's voice, Jacob calling my name. The bees rose
like sunlit dust.

Jacob's dark boots were by my face. "What the hell are you
doing on the floor?"

I squeezed the gardening gloves in my hand and sat up.

"Are you all right? Did you fall?" When I didn't answer, he
said, "I'm seriously worried about you."

Maybe I wasn't all right. That was a possibility. I looked at
my arms, at where the bees had been. I looked to the ceiling.
They weren't there. I sat up. "I'm sorry."

"What are you doing in here?"

"I was getting a trowel." I showed him the gloves as
though that helped explain why I'd been lying on the floor
of the shed.

As Jacob pulled me to my feet, I looked once more for
the bees. There was no sign of them. Had I imagined them? I
felt caught between two worlds, one where I was special, some
magical beekeeper, and another where I did what I was told.
I kept the house neat, made dinner, spread my thighs as wide
as they would go. I was a trapeze artist walking a tightrope.
On one side just beneath me bubbled the oblivion of living
like this forever, this angry man never letting me forget that I
was always wrong. I wasn't sure exactly when it started, when
it became clear that I was no longer in control of my life, that

everything, including my own happiness, depended on Jacob's happiness. One day, it just was. I think that the seeds were planted early on. Maybe I should've known that something was seriously amiss when he said that no professor could teach him anything. Maybe I should've known when he was rude to Cora's doctor. Maybe I was so caught up with the idea of marriage and normalcy that I lost the ability to distinguish between cruelty and kindness. All I knew for sure was that two years into our marriage, I was sorry every day for everything. I could do nothing right. I said the wrong thing, looked at him the wrong way.

Because I was always wrong, he shoved me. It was my fault. I shouldn't infuriate him so. Then, he put his hand to my throat because I wouldn't shut up. I said the wrong thing again. He said, "If you really love me, you'll stop pushing my buttons."

I tried, and I failed. When I fought back, he laughed. Later, he cried, "Why do you make me act this way? All I want to do is love you." And some part of me believed him. Maybe I'd heard him tell me too many times that I was to blame, or maybe it was easier to believe him than fight back. And there were no bruises, not on the outside, and I was too embarrassed to tell anyone.

Either way, two years in, I had mastered walking on eggshells. I listened for agitation in his voice, for sarcasm. I said whatever I thought Jacob wanted to hear. I agreed with everything he said, backtracked and apologized if I upset him.

I accepted responsibility for his anger, found good hiding spots, the shed and sometimes the pantry. I thought about leaving him, but my life, the eggshells, took on a surprising normalcy, and the more time that passed, the easier it was to keep doing what I was doing, to pretend to be someone I wasn't, to tolerate behavior that Jacob argued "is perfectly normal. A man loses his temper. Just because your father's a pansy doesn't mean every man is."

But then, holding my balancing stick, my feet wobbly on the tightrope, was the other side: the soft sweet side where Betty and the bees gathered. In that spot, there was cool water and sunlight, and I could be myself. Only I didn't think I deserved that—happiness. I was confused. I teetered.

In the summer of 1973, Jacob and Early Bird built a workshop on our land. They constructed the building out of two-by-fours and aluminum siding. Jacob's salvage business had developed into a furniture repair, refinishing, and restoration operation. He and Early Bird scoured antique malls, estate sales, thrift stores, and flea markets for battered antique pieces to repair and sell for a profit. Early Bird did most of the hardware repair, while Jacob did the sanding and ding repair. I worked eight to ten hours a day with the stains and lacquers, so I saw less of Betty. She was the other reason I hadn't run home to Maryville. I liked being around her. I never told her about

Jacob's tantrums. That's what I called them, "tantrums." It was just another secret to keep.

In July, Betty telephoned while I was in the kitchen getting a glass of water. She said, "Tell Jacob that you're taking the day off. Even God took a day off. We need some girl time. And wear your bathing suit. We're going to have some fun."

"Yes, ma'am." I was excited.

I went upstairs. Jacob was shaving. "Hey, can I take the day off?"

"What for?"

"Betty and I are going to do something fun."

"Are you shopping again?"

"No. It sounds like we're going swimming."

"You know I don't like her," he said. "What time will you be home?"

"Before dark."

"Don't be late." As I headed to the bedroom for my bathing suit, Jacob said, "I love you." He was being nice. I never knew which Jacob I'd encounter. I turned to see him in the doorway. "You didn't say, 'I love you too.'"

"I love you too. I'm going to get dressed."

"I'm just making sure you love me."

I waited for him to go back to the bathroom. Then, I put on my only swimsuit, a black-and-white-striped one-piece that was saggy in the rear. It reminded me of my childhood, how Sparky's sisters had made fun of me at the pool. I smiled before heading downstairs to pack sandwiches. Then, I saw Betty's convertible through the kitchen window. I called to Jacob, "I'll see you this afternoon."

"If I'm here."

He wanted me to stop, turn around, and rethink my decision. I was supposed to ask, *Where are you going?* but I didn't. I wouldn't. I ran outside carrying an old bread bag filled with peanut-butter-and-jellies.

Betty had a fancy wicker picnic basket in the back seat. "I thought of lunch," she said.

"Me too." I got into the front seat. I was excited. It'd been another long, hot dull summer.

Betty said, "I like your sunglasses."

"Thanks. Early Bird spotted them at some thrift store and thought they'd suit me."

"They really do. So did Jacob give you any shit about taking the day off?"

"Nope. None."

Betty glanced at my hands. "Your fingernails are black, Gloria."

"Well, the stain doesn't come out, you know. I can't do anything about it. They're not dirty."

"Oh, I know."

I slipped them under my thighs. "Where are we going?"

"To one of my favorite places, a place I used to go with my mom."

"I feel special."

"You are." I hadn't seen Betty since May. I'd been busy staining furniture, and she'd been busy at the restaurant. Every Saturday afternoon, she went to Durham. She didn't come back until Monday night or Tuesday morning. I knew, because I'd tried to call her on quite a few Sundays, when I felt low and lonely, when I wanted to tell someone that I was unhappy.

As we were driving, she said, "I'm not going to Durham for a while."

"How come? Is the restaurant too busy?" This was good news.

"No. It's not that."

"What is it?"

From the passenger seat, I could see that Betty was upset. She swallowed hard, then clicked her tongue against the roof of her mouth. "I was actually dating someone. Her name was Susie. We went to Chapel Hill together. We were just friends, but then last year, we started dating." I now understood why Betty wasn't married. I also wished that I wasn't married.

"I'm sorry," I said.

"She met someone else. At least that's what she said, but I don't think that's it. I don't think she's telling the truth."

"I'm sorry." There was nothing else to say.

"I hope it doesn't freak you out that I'm a lesbian."

"Not at all," I said. "Of course not." But I *was* freaked out.

216

She was like me. Beautiful, sweet Betty was like me. It was bittersweet for obvious reasons.

As we drove farther from Greeley, the flatland turned woody. There were hills. The road curved. We neared a thicket of briars, and Betty said, "This is Wampus Creek." She parked the car and grabbed the picnic basket. She wore a red-and-white gingham dress and red flip-flops. Her hair was in pigtails. There was a state park sign and beyond it a wooded trail. I followed Betty down the path.

I said, "You still have other friends in Durham though, right?"

"I do," she said, "but it's weird. They only just found out that Susie and I were more than friends, and now that we've split up, I don't know how it's going to be. I don't want anyone to feel like they have to take a side. It didn't end well. Susie and I aren't speaking."

"Even if I knew Susie, I'd take your side."

She said, "You're so sweet, Gloria," which made me smile.

The path ended at a creek. Betty said, "I know it looks shallow, but right out there in the middle"—she pointed—"it's about five feet deep. And you see that rock?"

I nodded.

"We can eat lunch right there."

Betty pulled her dress over her head. "It's best if you wear your shoes. Sometimes there's broken glass or you can get cut on a rock. Can you tell I've been here a lot?"

Betty wore a black high-waist two-piece bathing suit,

and I tried not to stare at her cleavage or her thighs, which were a milky white. I stepped into the creek and felt my way toward the rock. Then, suddenly, I went under. Betty jumped in beside me. I grabbed onto her. "Can you swim?" she asked.

"I can swim." I was treading water. "It just got deep all of a sudden."

She laughed. "I love spending time with you, Gloria. You're funny."

I said, "Since you're not going to Durham as much, maybe we can spend more time together."

"Absolutely."

As long as I didn't tell her that I liked her, how I liked her . . . As long as I didn't touch her, kept my hands to myself, I could be around her, and I needed her. I couldn't afford to lose her.

We floated under the sunlit trees, and I imagined telling Betty the truth about my past, about Isabel and Sheff. *I don't love Jacob. I burned the old Gloria. I got married. I'm supposed to be just like everybody else, but I'm not. I never will be.*

We climbed onto the rock and Betty pulled out the turkey-and-cheese sandwiches she'd made. She passed me one. I tugged at the bottom of my bathing suit. Betty smiled before taking a bite of her sandwich. "We really should go shopping more often." She eyed my sad suit.

"You're sort of a bitch, Betty."

She laughed, nearly choking on her sandwich. "At least you know the real me."

We finished our sandwiches. The sun felt warm on my back. It was the best day I'd had in months. After we ate, Betty lay on the rock, her back arched, her sunglasses perched on her nose. I caught myself admiring her waist, the line that ran from her belly button to her breasts, and those breasts, the whiteness of them, how they lolled to either side of her chest, how one was slightly larger than the other. Her wet brown hair was splayed on the rock. Her toes were painted red. She said, "Susie was really uptight. We never should've dated. I guess it was just easy because we'd known each other." She thought for a minute. "What was I thinking? Jesus, but she voted for fucking Nixon."

I said, "I was going to vote for Bobby Kennedy, but then he was assassinated, and I just sort of gave up on politics. I wouldn't vote for Humphrey because he wasn't going to get us out of Vietnam, and I wouldn't vote for Nixon for the same reason. I don't even watch the news or read the papers anymore. It's too depressing."

"Don't give up, Gloria. How old are you?"

"Twenty-four."

"I'm twenty-nine. You can't give up on the world. That I know for sure."

"I guess."

Betty sat up. "In addition to supporting Nixon, Susie was

never okay with being gay. It took months before she could tell our friends that we were a couple, and even afterwards, she was uncomfortable. She thought she was committing a sin."

I remembered Belmont. I understood how Susie must've felt. I wondered if she'd been locked up.

Betty said, "She was raised Baptist, and I think a big part of her wants to get married and have kids and do what her parents and her church want her to do. I never pressured her about anything, but whenever we were together, it was like she felt guilty for simply being herself. It's hard to explain."

"It sounds like it's really for the best that you two split up."

"I just want to be happy," Betty said. "I look at my mom, and it hits me too fucking hard that I only get this one life. I gotta do it right. Live every moment like it's my last." She bit into a green apple. Juice dribbled down her chin and I reached out and wiped it off, putting my finger to my mouth. Betty tucked her knees close to her body. She said, "That's the thing I don't get. How could she be dating someone else? She's not, not unless it's a man."

I had no answers. "Do you love her?"

"No."

"Then, just forget it."

"Sometimes, I wonder if I even know what love is."

"I knew someone who said the same thing." I lay back on the rock, my head touching Betty's, the dappled light streaming through the trees. "I'm really glad that we're friends." There was nothing else I could say.

Betty said, "You're going to regret that when I'm calling you up whining because I miss Susie."

A bee flew over my hand. Betty said, "Be careful."

I laughed. "I'm not afraid of bees. They've got way more important things to do than bother humans. Do you know that bees have to beat their wings something like two hundred beats per second to hover over a flower? Do you know that they die if they sting you?"

"You're into bees."

"I guess." The sun was setting, and I rolled onto my stomach. The gray rock felt cool. "I've been stung twice. The first time I was seven years old. My mother had gone into premature labor." I drummed my fingers on the rock. "She lost two babies." I paused for a second. "Just tell me to shut up if I'm talking too much."

"No," Betty said, "keep talking."

"The second time was during my wedding ceremony. I was just about to say, 'I do,' and a bee stung me behind my ear. Both times, I kept it to myself. I never told anyone that I was stung." I was thinking out loud. "There are all these myths— Native American, African, and Celtic—about how bees are symbolic of birth and creativity; they can be spirits traveling from one world to the next."

Betty said, "Have you always been this far-out?"

I smiled. "I guess so."

"Does Jacob know about the bees?"

"Nah."

"Is everything okay with you two?"

Here was my chance to tell the truth, but I didn't. "Sure. Fine."

"I'm sorry about your mom's babies."

"She was depressed for a long time, but she's better now."

Betty said, "My mother has no idea who I am this week. I went to see her yesterday, and she said, 'I don't know where I am, Julie.' She called me Julie. I don't know who Julie is. Then she said, 'Is it safe here? I'm worried it's not safe here.' I told her that it was safe."

Betty looked like she was going to cry. I crawled across the rock and hugged her. She felt soft and wet in my arms. My chest was pressed against hers. I didn't want to let go. I didn't think she wanted to let go either.

A few weeks later, Jacob was in Raleigh for the night. Betty came over. We were drinking a bottle of Chardonnay. I pulled her into the pantry to show her the beehive situated between the wood lath and the exterior of the house. I said, "It's a secret," my finger to my lips.

"Most people would call somebody and have it removed or torch it."

"I'm not most people."

"Don't I know that."

"It's like a universe right there."

"And you're not scared?"

"I told you they don't care about me. They're busy protecting their queen, producing honey. I'm irrelevant."

"And no one else knows?"

"Just you."

"And now I feel special."

And she was.

part three

I know he's dead! . . . I can still like him, though, can't I? Just because somebody's dead, you don't just stop liking them, for God's sake—especially if they were about a thousand times nicer than the people you know that're *alive* and all.

—J. D. Salinger, *The Catcher in the Rye*

26

In early December, Jacob told me that we were spending Christmas at my parents' house. Unbeknownst to me, he and my father had been corresponding. Jacob had written, explaining that it was hard to remain a purist when he was making money hand over fist. He bragged that his restoration business was booming. I knew that we were broke. At least, I never saw any of this reported income.

On the telephone, my father said, "It sounds like you two are doing quite well for yourselves. Jacob says business is good."

"I guess so." I didn't know what else to say. "I'm looking forward to seeing you at Christmas."

"Same here. Your mother is ecstatic."

Whether we were making money or not, the business kept Jacob busy. He was always in Raleigh going to estate sales and flea markets, buying more furniture. I liked that he wasn't home. It meant that Betty could come over. Sometimes, we watched television. Sometimes, we listened to music. Sometimes, we just talked. Her mother was going rapidly downhill.

On December 21, Jacob and I left for my parents' house. Oscar went to Betty's. On the drive, Jacob talked about the estate sales he'd been to in Raleigh. He said, "There's a greater potential for bigger profit if we buy higher-end furniture. The pieces we're restoring are fine, but I'd like to get into a more lucrative bracket. I'm thinking it might be a good idea to bring in investors."

I looked down at my black-stained hands. "Uh-huh."

"I wonder if your parents would want to invest."

"I don't know." But I did know. This was part of a ruse. We weren't doing well. He was after my parents' money. Jacob kept talking about how our business was a great opportunity for anyone with common sense, how my father would be foolish not to invest. I didn't want to fight, so I stayed quiet. Eventually, I fell asleep. I woke just before the exit for Maryville.

On Christmas Day, my parents invited the Babineauxs and Uncle Eddie to the house. Uncle Eddie was in town for the holiday. Since we were staying at the house, Uncle Eddie was staying at a motel close by.

Gwen, Eugene, and Uncle Eddie arrived around five. Gwen and I sat close together on the sofa, drinking hot toddies. She asked about our restoration business. I figured that Jacob had already hit Eugene up for an investment. I told her, "We're not being very purist since I spend all day inhaling fumes. And I don't know anything about the money side of it." Then, I told Gwen about Betty, about her mom and the forgetfulness, the nursing home. I told her about Wampus Creek, about the blue dress Betty had bought for my birthday, but I didn't tell her that Betty was gay. If I'd told her that part, she would have known straightaway that I was attracted to and most surely in love with Betty Jenkins.

When I caught myself talking solely about Betty, I changed the subject. I switched to Poppy. "She's the biggest gossip. I think she might actually open people's mail."

"No!"

"I wouldn't be surprised. She should write a gossip column. She seems to know all the dirt on everyone in town."

The men sat talking at the kitchen table. I hoped Jacob wasn't pitching them too hard. Here was a man who didn't want to take charity from anyone unless it suited him.

I was making a drink when Eddie came up, resting his hands on my shoulders. "We need to catch up."

I turned to see him. "Where's your Honey my mother told me about?"

"Walk outside with me."

I grabbed my coat. Snow blew through the blackness.

The patio was slippery. Uncle Eddie took my arm. "For the record," he said, "you and your shit-for-brains husband can come down to Vilano Beach anytime and meet Honey in person. She's with her kids in Miami this week. They're grown. She's a grandma."

"Don't call Jacob a shit-for-brains. God! You haven't changed." I stuck out my tongue to catch a flake. We walked toward the pines.

"I'm sober," he said, "usually. More than before."

"I stand corrected. That is a big change."

"I know!" He patted his own back. "But seriously, Gloria, I don't like him. He's a prick."

"You don't know him."

"I just spent an hour listening to him. He's an arrogant prick. He's so full of himself, I'd say he's got some kind of serious fucking mental problem. What's it called? There's a name for it."

"What?"

"I'm thinking." He snapped his fingers. "Delusions of grandeur. I think that's it, like he thinks he's better than everybody else."

Uncle Eddie had just psychologically analyzed my husband, and he'd pretty much hit the nail on the head. "He's a good guy." He wasn't, but he was my husband. I ought to defend him.

Uncle Eddie shook his head. "He's a fucking shit-for-brains." We walked farther on. "All I'm saying is I don't like him. I don't trust him. Get rid of him."

"That's all you're saying?"

"That's it. Nothing to it." Then, Eddie changed the subject. "Honey is a great woman. I really want you to meet her. You'll like her. She's not a shit-for-brains. You only make that mistake once."

"Maybe next year I'll come down."

"Come down anytime. We've got room."

"Can I bring the arrogant prick?"

"If you must."

That night, Jacob and I climbed into my girlhood bed. It was the same as I remembered. I watched the snow fall outside the window. I didn't feel particularly grown up, no more than I had ten years prior. Jacob slid his hand between my thighs. I wasn't in the mood. I rolled onto my side, my back to him. Uncle Eddie was right. I'd seriously fucked up.

On the drive home to Greeley, Jacob said, "Why did you move my hand when I tried to touch you? You're my wife! I'm allowed to touch you."

"I was tired."

Then, he didn't say anything for a few minutes. "Your father said no. He said that he didn't want to invest until he saw our books. I guess that's reasonable enough. I just figured that since I'm his son-in-law and you're his daughter that he'd want to help us. We're family."

I said, "Why don't you ask your father?"

"He doesn't have any money. You know that, Gloria."

Then, we didn't talk for over an hour.

The snow disappeared, replaced by brown slush. I thought that I should've stayed in Maryville, but my home was in Greeley, with Betty. I missed her. I wondered how things had gone with her mother. I'd done a lot of thinking in Maryville. After we were home, I would tell Jacob that I wanted a divorce. Only one person on my mother's side of the family had ever gotten divorced, and he'd been shunned. I had vague memories of being at my grandparents' house. Maybe I was four or five, and this man had come down the stairs. I remembered my nana and pa looking up. My mother did the same, and he'd disappeared back up the stairs. There were whispers. Later, my mother would tell me that he'd caught his wife cheating, but just the same, divorce wasn't an option. Somehow, he was partly to blame for her infidelity, but I knew that my parents wouldn't shun me. My marriage wasn't technically a sacrament. There'd been no Mass.

Considering Jacob's temper, I'd have to be ready to leave right after I told him. I'd have to make sure that he hadn't been drinking. His temper was worse when he drank. Then, after I was separated and divorced, I would tell Betty how I felt about her. It would take time, but it would be worth it. I would be happy. Riding home to Greeley, I was hopeful.

27

I MISSED MY PERIOD. IT was the third one I'd missed. I'd chalked it up to irregularity, to being too thin, to inhaling too many lacquers and stains. Then, Betty brought it up. "Did you ever get your period?"

"No, but I'm sure I will."

"You're pregnant."

"No, I'm not."

"I bet so."

I hadn't been home a week. She insisted on taking me to see her obstetrician-gynecologist in Washington City. She got me an appointment for that day. Jacob was in Durham on business. I was planning to ask for a divorce soon, very soon.

Betty picked me up. I didn't want to be pregnant. I wanted to tell Betty the truth about who I was and how I felt.

Betty drove the twenty miles to the doctor's office. It was a squat brick building beside a towering hospital. "Whatever happens," she said, "it'll be good." Before I saw the doctor, his nurse, Janelle, did a blood and urine test. Then, she took me and Betty to a room to wait for the doctor and the results. "It might be a while," she said. "Dr. Donato delivered a baby this morning, so he's a little behind schedule." She pulled the door shut.

Betty said, "Are you excited?"

I shook my head. "I feel nauseous."

Betty came over and patted my thigh. I admired her red fingernails.

"I don't think I'm good at being married. I really don't think I'd be a good mother."

"Darlene said that Jacob hit her. I didn't know if she was lying. He doesn't hit you, right?"

"No. Of course not." He'd pushed me, choked me, berated and bullied me, but he'd never hit me.

"Thank God. Probably nobody is good at marriage, Gloria. Everybody says it takes work, but I know you'd be a good mother."

Then, the doctor opened the door and Betty took my hand in hers. Dr. Donato wore a long white coat. It was partway open. He wore a green seersucker necktie and khaki pants. "Mrs. Blount, it's nice to meet you." He shook my hand.

"You too."

"Hi, Betty."

"Hi, Dr. Donato."

He looked at my chart. "You are most certainly without a doubt pregnant." He smiled. "I hope this is good news."

I was speechless. Betty said, "Yay!" and clapped her hands. "I'll be an aunt."

"You told Janelle that you weren't sure, but you thought your last menstrual period was sometime in September. Have you had any nausea?" the doctor asked.

"Right now."

"What about breast tenderness?"

"Yes, but I kept thinking that maybe my period was about to start."

"The good news is that you've been through what some women consider the toughest trimester."

"What does that mean?"

"You're already three months along. You have about six to go. Probably twenty-six to twenty-eight weeks. So, what we're going to do now is, I'm going to ask Betty to leave the room, and I'm going to do a pelvic exam." I looked around. There was a window, metal blinds pulled shut. I felt warm. The room was too confined. "You'll be fine," he said. He slid the metal stirrups out. Betty said, "I'll be right outside."

"I don't know if I'm ready to have a baby."

"A lot of women say that. Don't worry. Now I just need you to lie back and relax your legs for me."

"I like your tie."

He touched it and looked down. "Thank you."

"I used to sell ties."

"Here. Scooch down for me. Try and relax. It's easier that way."

"It's cold."

"Sorry about that. Just taking a peek," he said.

I stared at the ceiling, trying not to tense up, which was impossible. I couldn't have a baby. I didn't know how to be a mother. Jacob didn't know how to be a father.

"Everything looks good. The cervix changes color when you're pregnant."

"What color is it?"

"It's a little blue."

"That's weird."

"It's exactly what we want. It's caused by the increase in blood flow." He removed the speculum. "You're going to experience a lot of changes. You might become short of breath. You should avoid doing anything too strenuous. Basically, listen to your body." I sat up. Dr. Donato was bald. He had a round face and a kind smile. "I'll send you home with some information, and I'll want to see you back in two months. You can schedule an appointment with Tammi before you leave. Do you have any questions for me?"

"Who's Tammi?"

"My receptionist. You saw her when you checked in."

"Right. One more thing: my mother had a couple miscarriages, and then she had twins prematurely and they didn't make it."

"Oh, Gloria," he said. "You're not your mother. So far, everything looks good. I'll see you every two months and then every month and then every week as we get closer to your due date. Stay positive."

"Yes, sir." I needed to cry. I was overwhelmed. I didn't know how to be a mother. I'd had a plan and it did not include a baby.

"You get dressed, and I'll see you soon. You're going to be great."

I wasn't great. I was pregnant. I didn't say very much after we got in the car. I touched my stomach where I thought the baby must be. *Can I get an abortion? I'll tell Betty that I miscarried. A baby will complicate everything. Jacob will want to see it. To be a father.* I felt like I was going to throw up. "Betty, can you stop?" She pulled off to the side of the road on Route 614. I pushed my door open and ran toward the ditch. A cold wind blew out of the north. A sixteen-wheeler roared past, the force whipping my hair. The ground was hard, my breath visible. Steam rose up from where I got sick. I wiped my mouth with the back of my hand and returned to Betty's car. As I pulled the door closed, I began to cry.

Betty looked at me. "It's going to be okay, Gloria."

What was I going to do? I knew that I could never go through with getting an abortion. There was a life inside me. I wouldn't snuff it out. Betty's car was warm, the engine running. A van drove past.

I wiped my face with my coat sleeve. "I don't know. It's just a lot to take in. I guess I'm in shock."

"Everything's going to be all right. There's nothing to worry about. I'm here." She cleared her throat. "Do you think Jacob will be happy? Are you worried about how he's going to feel?"

"No. I think he'll be happy. I guess I'm just overwhelmed."

Betty pulled back onto Route 614 toward Greeley. "I'm here. Don't forget it. I'm not going anywhere."

By the time I got home, it was after five o'clock. Jacob was in the workshop, using the sander. I wasn't going to bother him. Oscar followed me into the kitchen, where I put the pregnancy brochures on the table and went to the pantry. I needed to make dinner. I pulled the light cord and looked up. There were a few straggler bees not hibernating. They'd probably die soon. I pointed at my stomach. "Baby," I said, before pulling a can of green beans off the shelf. "I knew you'd be excited." The bees were hardly moving. I pulled the light cord. "Good night."

I took a package of hot dogs from the fridge and, nauseated, sat at the table, my head in my hands. I was still wearing my winter coat. *I don't want to have a baby. I was careful not to have sex when I was ovulating nearly all the time except for when Jacob insisted. I was really careful. Fuck.*

Jacob tromped into the kitchen, his brown jacket smelling of cigarette smoke. I reached for the pregnancy brochures. "What's that?" he said, taking hold of my wrist.

"Huh?"

"What you got?"

I handed them to him. Oscar settled under the table, his snout on my foot. Jacob looked at the titles: *How to Have a Healthy Baby* and *You're Eating for Two.* "Who's pregnant?" He looked at me. "Are you pregnant, Gloria? Are you?" He was waiting. His dark eyes wide. "Is it you?"

"Yes."

"Yes!" He pounded the table with his fist. "Thank God! I was getting worried that my seed was no good. We've been having sex for three years, I mean, I figured maybe one of us was defective. Hot damn! Did you see a doctor?"

"Today," I told him.

"Are you all right? When are you due?"

"Six months about. July."

He took my face in his hands and kissed me. "You look tired."

"I am."

"You go up to bed. I'll make dinner tonight."

He went to the sink and washed his hands. "Oh, Gloria, thank you. I'm going to do everything right that my dad did wrong. Just wait until Big Mama hears. And I need to call Early Bird."

That night, I dreamed the bees flew together, taking the shape of Sheff. I knew with certainty that it was him, even as his figure pulsed and vibrated, golden bits of him flying here and there. I knew it was Sheff how I knew when I fell in a dream that I'd wake before the pavement because it's not the end that's unbearable. It's the flail, the arms and legs waving but going nowhere, the anticipation and dread, the fall. With this knowledge, I went to Sheff, to hold him or some piece of him, and as I drew near, the bees parted; the form dispersed. When I stepped back, the bees flew together. I shouted over the hum: "I'm having a baby." He was in there somewhere, but I couldn't sense what he was feeling, couldn't touch him. I screamed over the buzz, "I'm having a baby!" When he didn't respond, I tried again to hold him, but my arms and legs and voice scattered the bees. They didn't fly back, and I woke feeling sad.

I'm having a baby, darling Sheff.

I'm not getting divorced. I cried before I got out of bed. Downstairs, I found a note in the kitchen. *Be home by six. Take it easy. I love you. J*

After I had coffee and toast, I telephoned my parents. "We're having a baby!" I tried to sound happy, but my mother must've detected the sadness in my voice because after her initial joyful squeals and acknowledgment that she'd be a nana, she asked, "Are you all right? You don't sound good."

"I'm just emotional."

"That's understandable. Oh, but it's going to be wonderful."

"It doesn't seem real to me."

"And it won't, maybe not until you're holding that baby."

In the weeks and months that followed, Betty phoned every morning to ask how I was feeling. In truth, I felt stuck, but I was well practiced in the art of pretending to be what I was not, so while I trudged through my pregnancy, everyone around me celebrating my growing girth, I smiled and feigned celebrating right along with them. I bought "fat clothes" at the thrift store and shopped for the baby's nursery with Betty.

Jacob was generally agreeable and spent two to three nights a week in Raleigh, reportedly searching antique markets and estate sales for more furniture even though the workshop was full, the bulk of our supply unfinished. Early Bird worked eight to nine hours a day most days. I didn't understand why Jacob was never home, but because I appreciated his absence, I kept my mouth shut. Then, one afternoon in late March, while I was out sweeping the front porch, Jacob pulled up in his truck. I saw Early Bird rush from the workshop, his hands in fists. He was shouting. "What's going on with you, brother? I'm doing all the work because you can't keep your dick in your pants!"

Jacob said, "Keep it down."

"You know what I'm saying."

Then, they saw me standing on the porch. Jacob asked me, "Do you need something?"

"No."

"Are you eavesdropping?" He cupped his hand around his ear. "Are you spying?"

"No. I was sweeping."

"Go inside, Gloria."

I did as I was told. I never said anything about what Early Bird had said because I was still well practiced at walking on eggshells, and Jacob would have had some excuse or explanation for Early Bird's claim, and then Early Bird would have been at my door defending Jacob, so I said nothing. I kept trudging. My mother sent a white crib from Sears. Gwen sent a star mobile. Betty painted a circus-themed border along the floor and ceiling. She filled the nursery with stuffed elephants and giraffes, and Early Bird gave me an antique dresser that he'd refinished especially for the baby. After he moved the dresser into the nursery, I thanked him. Then he seemed to summon up courage. He scrunched up his face. "Can I touch your belly?"

"The baby's not moving yet."

"I know, but can I touch it?"

"Of course." I started to lift up my shirt, but he stopped me.

"Like this is just fine." His voice twanged like a guitar. He put his hand on my shirt and smiled. "Wow."

I nodded in agreement.

"If you ever need anything, you can count on me."

"Thank you."

"I mean it."

I knew he meant it.

In April, the bees buzzed like mad, leaving their hive to seek out pollen. They often trailed me across the lawn, into the shed, and even upstairs to my bedroom, but they fled when anyone else was around.

Big Mama knitted a white blanket, and it lay folded on a blue recliner that Betty had shipped from Goldsboro. Late at night when I couldn't sleep, I went to the nursery, the floorboards creaking underfoot, and I sat in the recliner with the blanket over my belly. I tried to imagine what it would be like with a baby, another whole person, in this very room, but it was impossible to conceive.

The first time the baby kicked, I was drinking iced tea in Betty's apartment. It was the strangest, most amazing feeling. The baby was really real. It took a kick to make him or her real. I took Betty's hand, sliding it right and left and up and down, my belly like a drum. We sat there all afternoon feeling for the little thumps. *I want my baby to live.* That same night, I dreamed of the bees. They were buzzing through the pines behind my parents' house. I trailed them. They were moving faster and faster, and I was chasing, but we ran a loop back to my parents' house. I could never catch up.

28

It was July 3, 1974, a Wednesday. I was home alone washing dishes when the phone rang. I wiped my hands on a dish towel and picked up. It was my mother. She said, "I'm not giving any speeches tomorrow."

"What?"

"At the party . . . no speeches this year."

"That's a big step. Are you sure? You always give a speech."

"Not this year. And my new college friends are coming."

"Do you think Maria Montefusco will be jealous?"

"Of what?"

"Your new friends."

"Probably." She giggled. "It'll be good."

"So, no speech, really?"

"I told your father that he should make one, or at least a toast."

"Nice."

"That's what he said."

"Do you think he'll talk about salt?"

"Most likely."

I laughed. "Saltines have been really good to me lately."

"I had to call and tell you. We're going to miss you tomorrow."

"I'll miss you too."

"I love you."

"I love you too."

I hung up the phone and returned to my dishes.

I was halfway through the stack when I felt a sharp pain in my lower back. I nearly dropped a glass. "Fuck." The pain subsided and I finished the dishes. Dr. Donato had said, "Don't rush to the hospital at the first bit of discomfort. They'll just send you home. Try and relax and breathe through the contractions. The first baby usually takes between twelve and twenty-four hours of labor. I know what I'm talking about. I've been doing this for two decades."

After I dried and put the dishes away, I went upstairs and stood in the nursery. I was getting close. I imagined that maybe tomorrow I'd be ready to go to the hospital. Throughout the day, I had waves of discomfort in my lower back. I took deep breaths and relaxed into them. The pain came and it went, and I tried to stay busy. In the afternoon, I decided to clean the tub.

The bathroom was a small space, and the basket-weave tiles were cracked around the commode. After a short time down on my knees, the pain was worse, and I got to my feet, bracing myself against the sink. *Fuck!* One of the honeybees flew into the room. It buzzed around the ceiling, then circled my face before leaving.

I made my way downstairs. Jacob and Early Bird were off somewhere. I wasn't sure where. It was time to go to the hospital. I couldn't wait any longer. I picked up the phone and dialed Betty's number. While I was waiting for her to pick up, a flurry of bees flew from the pantry. They were larger bees with big dark eyes. Drones. They flew toward the ceiling.

Betty said, "Hello."

"I need you." I stared at the drones, their big eyes staring back.

"Is it time?"

"Yes, please."

"I'm there." She hung up, and I leaned back in the kitchen chair, trying to remember what I'd read about breathing. I couldn't remember much of anything. The drones hovered by the plaster ceiling before the hive emerged, converging, a bright humming golden ball swirling above me. I was in awe of them.

When I heard Betty's car door open and shut, the bees flew back to the hive. She opened the kitchen door. There was no trace of them. "It's time to have a baby, right? Is that what we're talking about?" Her hair twisted, pinned high up in a bun, she was ready to get to work. "Let's do it."

Betty darted upstairs for my suitcase. Then, she telephoned Washington City Hospital to let them know that we were on our way. "After we get there," she told me, "I'll try to locate Jacob. I'll call Big Mama."

"Call my mother."

"I will. Oh, do you want to drive?"

"Oh my God." I swatted at her. "No, I can't drive right now."

"That's why you love me. Because I'm funny like you."

Betty drove fast along the backcountry roads, illegally passing multiple cars. I said, "Don't kill us."

"I'm not killing anybody, but you don't want to give birth in my Bug. Correct?"

"Correct."

Betty sped beneath the ambulance-only underpass of the hospital and pulled the parking brake. I flew forward, my hand on the dashboard.

Betty got out of the car. "Help! My friend's having a baby."

A man wearing a dull green smock and identification badge came over. "You can't park here. You need to move your car."

"My friend's having a baby."

"I've got her."

Betty said, "Are you okay, Gloria?"

"I'm okay."

"I'm Ray," the man said. He wheeled me into the hospital, asking my name and date of birth. I answered him, but then I started to cry. "You're all right," he said. "You're in good hands."

At the admitting desk, a different man asked the same question, adding, "What's your pain on a scale of one to ten?"

"Fifteen."

The woman behind the desk said, "Get that one upstairs pronto. We're not having any babies down here." Another woman said, "She's one of Dr. Donato's. I've got her information." She put a band on my arm.

Then, I was wheeled upstairs to Labor and Delivery. I asked Ray, "Will my friend be able to find me?" Everything was happening too fast.

"There's only one Labor and Delivery floor." He wheeled me into a delivery room. "Just one second," he said, ducking back out.

Then, two nurses came into the room, one tall, one short. The shorter nurse handed me a gown. "Put this on. It ties in the back." She introduced herself. "I'm Maggie. How are you doing, honey?" She wore a starched cap and white uniform dress.

"I'm not sure." I had been trying not to think about my mother's twins, but then I did. I was full-term, but what if my baby didn't live? I couldn't go home empty-handed. Maggie and the taller nurse, Lisa, helped me onto the delivery table.

Lisa said, "Well, we're going to take a look. Scooch down

for me. Let's get you in these stirrups." She told Maggie, "She's already at seven."

"Dr. Donato missed two births last month."

Lisa said, "I'm going to call him now."

I said, "What's going on?"

"Everything's good on this end. You're doing great," Maggie said. "How's your pain?"

"Terrible. My back is killing me."

"I'm going to start an IV, and you're going to feel better soon. Make sure you don't push until we tell you. Hopefully, Dr. Donato will be here by then."

"What?!"

"I'm just kidding," she said. "He'll be here."

I wished that Betty was with me. I didn't want to do this alone. After Maggie started the IV, I felt a warmth fill my limbs, and then I felt like I'd peed myself. I was sure my water had broken in Betty's car, but I hadn't said anything. *Surprise, Betty.*

"You're doing really well," Maggie said. "How's your pain?"

"Not bad."

"Can you tell me a number between one and ten?"

"Six."

"Great! That's not too terrible."

Lisa came back into the room. She had whitish-blonde hair pulled back in a ponytail. "So, I didn't quite get him," she said to Maggie. "He knows he's on call, but he didn't pick up."

"What's going on?" I asked.

"Everything's fine," Maggie said. "This hospital is full of doctors just dying to deliver their first baby."

Lisa laughed, and the pain surged. I lurched forward, moaning.

Maggie said, "Remember, don't push."

"It hurts again."

"What's your number?" she asked.

"Fuck a number!"

Lisa said, "I'm going to check." I felt her gloved hand between my legs. "She's already eight easy."

Maggie said, "Okay."

"What's eight?"

"That's how many centimeters you're dilated."

I grabbed onto the belt of her nice uniform. "Where's Dr. Donato? I think it's time to have this baby." I lurched forward again.

Maggie said, "Don't push. It's not time."

Lisa said, "How many ccs did you give her?"

"Not enough. Where is that pompous asshole?"

Lisa said, "Are you thirsty? I'll get you some ice chips."

I was. "Please."

"You're doing great," Maggie said. She checked me again. "You're already at nine. You're really fast. How many children do you have?"

"This is my first."

"Wow!"

"I need to push," I said. Maggie went to the door and called to Lisa, "Forget the ice. It's nearly time." They both put on new gloves that popped at their wrists. Then they tied on surgical masks. Maggie said, "Check her."

"She's fast. She's ten."

"I hate Dr. Donato," Maggie said.

"He always does this shit."

Maggie said, "You are a warrior princess, Gloria. You are about to be a new mom. You can do anything. Are you ready?"

I grunted.

"Then, let's do this. When you feel like pushing, bear down like you're taking a big poop and push as hard as you can."

I pushed once, and then I fell back, panting. "You can do this," Lisa said. My feet were in the stirrups, but she took hold of both my hands and pulled me up, helping me to bear down.

Maggie said, "I see the head. One more push."

Lisa helped me push again.

"The baby's crowning. You're doing amazing, Gloria."

With the last push, I grabbed onto the backs of my knees and stayed there. I was going to push until my baby came out. Then, Maggie said, "It's a girl." She caught my baby and raised her up. She was slimy, her eyes closed, a shock of sticky white hair. Beautiful. Magnificent. Motionless.

I burst into tears. "She's not breathing. Why isn't she breathing? What's wrong with her?"

"It's okay." Lisa and Maggie were calm. How could they be calm?

I fell back, a deep sorrow building in my chest. I watched

as Lisa used a blue suction bulb in one of my baby's nostrils and then the other, wiping her face with a cloth. My baby took her first gurgled breath, then a second. Then, she wailed. She screamed, her mouth red and wide. Her voice full and loud. "My baby." The God that I'd lost when Sheff died came back with the force of gravity. He was bowling balls, anchors, and anvils pinning me down, clobbering me. I had a daughter. She was a miracle. I said, "Give me."

"We need to clean her up."

"Give her to me now!"

Maggie handed her to me. I was oblivious to everything that followed.

Maggie said, "We need to clean her up and get her Apgar, and we need to get you cleaned up. I think you might've torn a little." Then, Dr. Donato walked into the delivery room. He was scrubbed and ready to go.

Lisa rolled her eyes and shook her head and walked past him.

"Looks like you did a good job, Gloria."

"Thank you." I beamed.

Later that night, I woke up itchy from the drugs. I was clean, in a fresh grown, and in a new room. The moon outside my window was full. Maggie came in with my baby girl swaddled in a blanket. "Here's your mama," she said, handing her to me. "Do you have a name?" she asked.

"I have one in mind."

"Do you want to share?"

"Zelda."

"I like it."

"Thanks."

It was after eleven o'clock when Big Mama and Betty were allowed to visit. They'd already seen Baby Blount through the nursery glass. "She's beautiful," Big Mama said.

"I'm so proud of you," Betty said. "You did great. Wham bam, thank you, ma'am, they said. Way to go."

Big Mama said, "We got in touch with Early Bird, and he said that he'd find Jacob. I'm sure he'll be here first thing in the morning."

Betty and Big Mama were with me. I had a beautiful daughter. I had no complaints.

"Did you call my mother, Betty?"

"I did. She and your dad are over the moon. They're going to call you."

One of the nurses wheeled my baby into the room. I let Betty and Big Mama hold her. For now, her name was Baby Blount, but Zelda was starting to stick.

That night, after Betty and Big Mama had gone home and Zelda had been taken back to the nursery, I heard a buzzing sound. I turned to see a small hole to the right of the window unit air conditioner. Bees flew in through the hole, congregating and multiplying, spreading out along the windowsill. I sat up and watched their numbers grow. Their buzzing rivaled the air conditioner's hum. The bees circled one another, their buzzing morphing into something akin to words, his voice. They said, "I'm proud of you." I heard them, him.

I knew that it was crazy, but I felt him there. "I love you so much," I said. I remembered holding him. Then, I felt him beside me, and I slept.

29

BABY MADE THREE. I WASN'T leaving Jacob. I couldn't. What would I tell a judge?

> "I'm not happy in my marriage. Sometimes, he loses his temper. Sometimes he pushes me. He's put his hand over my mouth. No, your honor. I never told anyone."
>
> "Marriage takes work, Mrs. Blount. This man loves you. Have you ever called the police on him? Do you have any evidence to support that he's abusive?"
>
> "No, your honor."
>
> "Furthermore, how are you going to support your daughter? Where are you going to live? Is it really so bad at home, so bad that you would tear your family apart?"

Jacob would say, "You promised you'd never leave me. You said you loved me. You lied. You're a liar."

"Your honor," a lawyer would say, "Mrs. Ricci was institutionalized as an adolescent for being a homosexual. I don't see how she can be a responsible parent. For all we know, she might sexually molest her daughter."

These dialogues played in my head. I was stuck, but it was all right because I was in love with my baby.

At first, she slept between me and Jacob, but then Jacob moved down the hall to the spare bedroom. He came and went as he had before. When he was home, he said, "You're such a cutie," to Zelda, feeding her spoonfuls of rice cereal. He sometimes burped her, but he never changed a diaper. When she cried, he called, "Gloria, Zelda needs you." After dinner, he played "This little piggy went to market" with her, but then he left her to me. I bathed her and put her to bed. He was the man who came and went, making cooing sounds.

Everyone had warned me that the first year of motherhood would be tough, but it wasn't. It was bliss. My whole life, every second of every hour of every day, was spent caring for Zelda. If I'd had other responsibilities, life would've been incredibly difficult, but I had and wanted nothing else.

Her eyes were dark like Jacob's. Her hair was fair and curly like mine. She had rosy cheeks, pink lips, chubby thighs, and sweet fingers and toes that begged to be kissed. She rarely cried because I rarely put her down. When I took a bath, she took a bath. When I went to Betty's or Big Mama's, she came along. I wouldn't take her home to Maryville because I knew she'd get upset on the long car ride.

When my parents came to visit, I wouldn't let them do very much to help. "No, I don't need a break." "No, I don't want to go shopping with Betty, not without Zelda." "No, I don't need you to feed or bathe or put her to bed. I've got it." At night, I held her in my arms, Frank Sinatra on the turntable. "'Fly me to the moon,'" I sang. Instead of putting her in her crib, I took her to bed with me.

"Motherhood suits you," my father said.

My mother said, "You were such a sweet baby." My amazing mother was becoming the woman she'd always wanted to be. When Zelda was two months old, Mother received a teaching assistantship at a small liberal arts college.

In Greeley, Betty and I were raising Zelda. If I ever came clean and told anyone how I felt about Betty, I'd lose what we had. I was happy with how things were. I was with my two favorite people in the whole world, and when the weather was warm, the hive joined in. On hot summer afternoons, Betty picked me and Zelda up, and we went to Wampus Creek. Zelda loved the water. Betty had bought a green float that had a sling and it held Zelda aloft. She could splash and kick, floating around, spinning in the water. The honeybees and dragonflies zipped past. The late-afternoon sun filtered through the trees, dappling Betty's dark hair with white light.

Then one afternoon in late August, Betty was slurping

creek water in her mouth, spurting it up, playing fountain over Zelda's head, when I, without thinking, swam over and kissed her.

She swam away. I was in the light, and she was in the shade. She said, "What was that about, Gloria?" She was flustered. "What's wrong with you?"

"I'm sorry."

She stated the obvious. "You're married." Then, she added, "And you're not gay."

"I'm sorry. My hormones are all screwy, I think."

"Look, Gloria, I thought you knew this already. You don't have to be someone you're not when you're with me. I like you just how you are." She put her right hand at her neck, where a rash was breaking out. I'd upset her.

I wanted to tell her the truth: *I am gay, Betty, and I'm in love with you.* I wanted to kiss her again, but instead, I said, "I'm really sorry. You're my best friend." I made a funny face at Zelda to try and relieve the tension I'd created.

Betty said, "Is Jacob still working a lot? That's gotta be really tough on you."

It wasn't tough. It was a relief. I said, "It's fine. I'm sorry."

She said, "Are we okay?"

"Of course." The facade that was I, Gloria Blount, was cracking apart. There were big fissures. I was breaking open.

30

ZELDA SAT AT THE KITCHEN table, her face slick with butter and cinnamon. It was the fall of 1977. She was three. Time had passed quickly, and very little had changed. I heard Jacob's boots clomp down the steps.

"Do you want eggs?" I asked.

"None for me, but thanks." He kissed Zelda's forehead. "You're sticky," he said, pouring himself a cup of coffee. "I'm probably staying in Raleigh for the night. Another estate sale."

"Okay."

"Do you need anything from the market before I leave this afternoon?"

"We're good. We're going to the carnival tonight with Betty."

"Take Zelda on the Ferris wheel."

"As long as she's not scared."

"I'm never scared," she said. "You know that, Mommy."

Jacob kissed me on the cheek before he left.

Betty picked us up at six. Zelda wore her favorite red dress. She called it her fancy dress, which made me laugh. She liked tulle and taffeta, everything frilly, and when she said the word *fancy*, she elongated the *an* sound. She was terribly fancy, no question. She wore red cowboy boots. "I'm all ready," she said. "I want to see a polar bear and a lion."

"I don't think there will be polar bears or lions."

We got into Betty's car. Zelda sat in the back seat. She said, "But I want to see a big cat."

Betty put the car in reverse. "What about a kitten? Kittens are better than big cats."

"And a kitten," Zelda said.

"Aunt Betty can get you your very own kitten," Betty said. She had recently started feeding a colony of strays.

"No, thank you, Aunt Betty," I said.

"No, Mommy," Zelda said. "I would like to have a kitten."

I looked at Betty. I didn't need to say anything. We'd be getting a kitten. I knew it.

"Can we get the kitten tonight?"

"Soon," Betty said. Then we sang "Row, Row, Row Your Boat" on the way to the carnival. When we got to the fairgrounds, it was dark, but the area was strung with orange and white lights. We spotted the Ferris wheel and the Tilt-A-Whirl. Betty said, "The Tilt-A-Whirl is my favorite." We each took one of Zelda's hands, and swung her as we crossed the field heading toward the rides. "I think we have to buy tickets," Betty said. "I haven't been in a decade." We got our tickets at a squat concession stand and walked along a line of oaks, their leaves fallen. They crunched underfoot. The air smelled of fall.

We passed by a pumpkin patch, and Zelda said, "Let's see the pumpkins." It wasn't an actual patch, just an area roped off and strewn with pumpkins. It'd been a hot, dry summer. The pumpkins had been trucked in for the carnival and Halloween. I smelled popcorn and burning wood. Zelda walked methodically from pumpkin to pumpkin, trying to lift each one. By the sixth pumpkin, she succeeded. "I'll take this one," she said.

"We'll have to get it on the way out," I explained. "You don't want to carry it around the whole time, right?"

"I'll take this one," she repeated.

I said, "Let's set it over here so that no one else takes it."

She nodded, and followed me to the perimeter of the patch, setting it down. "Don't go anywhere," she warned the pumpkin. Betty tousled her curls. I watched the two of them before reaching out and grabbing Betty's hand. She smiled.

A south wind came out of nowhere, whipping up dust, cut grass, leaves, and trash. A crumpled handbill tumbled by my boot. I bent down and picked it up. The black letters were faded, but there was no mistaking the words *Madame Zelda, Fortune-Teller.* My mouth tasted chalky from the dust. I looked for Zelda, but she was gone. "Zelda?"

"She was just here," Betty said.

"Zelda!"

"Zelda!" Betty called.

I looked at Zelda's special pumpkin. I walked and then ran the perimeter of the pumpkin patch. Betty started asking everyone if they'd seen a little girl, red dress, blonde curls, red boots. "You can't miss her."

"Zelda!" I screamed. "Where are you?" The old handbill was balled in my fist. I asked the man who'd taken our pumpkin money if he'd seen Zelda.

"No, ma'am," he said, "but there's a lost-and-found for kids over there." He pointed toward the main tent. Betty and I jogged in that direction, shouting Zelda's name.

I told Betty, "She never runs off. Never!"

"I know."

"Do you think someone grabbed her?"

"She was right here."

"Then she was gone." I scanned the crowd. Betty looked back toward the patch. Then, I spotted Zelda's red tulle and boots. She stood before a yellow-and-orange-striped spired tent. A spotlight shone onto the image of a fortune-teller, her hands hovering over a crystal ball. I watched Zelda slip between two staked canvas flaps. Betty and I were already running toward her. "Wait, Zelda." We followed her between the canvas flaps, and immediately, my Zelda grabbed onto my thigh. "I got blown over here, Mommy."

Betty got down on her knees. "Thank God you're safe."

"The wind caught me, Aunt Betty."

There was a plywood placard painted in hues of purple, orange, and black, the image of a woman in a lavender shawl. *The one and only, the legendary Madame Zelda, Fortune-Teller.* "Look, Mommy," Zelda said, pointing to the sign. "It's a witch."

Betty said, "Never run off like that."

"I didn't run, Aunt Betty. The wind picked me up and blew me here like a leaf."

Then, I spotted Madame Zelda leaning against a post. The wind popped the tent flap at her feet. She wore a long purple skirt adorned with tiny mirrors. She had one arm folded at her waist, and she smoked a cigarette, the smoke rising, curling before her hook nose. I saw that her bony fingers were still covered with rings. Her hair was white, how I remembered, and her eyes were a dull brown. She flicked her cigarette, stubbing it with the toe of a purple boot, her skirt dragging the dirt, and approached us. "I've been waiting for you."

Betty whispered, "Do you know her?"

"I do," I said. "Can you stay with Zelda while we talk?"

Madame Zelda said, "Your little girl is telling the truth. The wind did carry her here."

Betty picked Zelda up. She clearly didn't think Madame Zelda was in her right mind. Probably, she'd grabbed our Zelda. "We'll be just outside," Betty said.

Madame Zelda said, "Take your time. The girl and I need to talk." By *the girl*, she meant me. Then, she said, "Wait," and reached out, taking my Zelda's face in her crooked fingers.

265

"You're a very pretty girl. The wind most certainly carried you to me."

"Thank you, ma'am," Zelda said.

"Now go have some fun while I talk to your mother."

Betty held tight to our Zelda. "We'll meet you out here."

Zelda said, "Let's find the kittens, Aunt Betty."

Madame Zelda said, "Follow me." I trailed her through two inner flaps. The table was just as I remembered, but now there was a crystal ball.

"Why have the ball if you don't use it?"

"It's part of the show. I think people like it." We sat in metal chairs. She drummed her long nails on the purple velvet shawl covering the table. I waited for her to pass the tin can. I reached into my pocket for a dollar. "I don't want your money," she said. "I just want to be done with you."

"I don't follow."

"What are you doing to the boy?"

"What boy?"

"What boy? Are you kidding me? The only boy, the boy with no fortune, Gloria. He torments me, and I've been tormented by the best of them, and when I say 'best,' I mean the worst of them—by murderers and rapists, the worst kind of people—but your boy is an innocent. He brings friends from the other side, good souls, and they harass me. You've done something to make the boy upset."

I was speechless.

"The boy wants you to be happy. He sends the bees to

me. They whisper, 'Tell the girl to stop blaming herself for the boy's death. Life is short.' The bees hound me. All manner of spirits come on behalf of that boy, and he comes with them. He spelled out that you'll be here at this carnival. He writes with green pollen like pixie dust." Madame Zelda smacked her hands on the table. "I am tired of him, of them. They come to me in dreams. They wake me up at night. That boy might be dead, but he's always close by, watching you. He wants me to show you the rivers that are my veins, and this skin on my arms, see how it hangs. The boy wants you to know that you have to honor who you are. Don't let anyone turn you into someone you aren't, Gloria. He says that Holden somebody didn't become a phony."

I started to cry.

"The boy and the bees are the most persistent spirits to come to me. 'Zelda, find her,' the boy compels me. There are many not of this world who watch over you."

"What am I supposed to do?"

"That, I don't know, girl. But clearly, the boy thinks you know what to do."

"I've been thinking about it."

"Well, good, because I need my peace. And like I said, none of us are long for this world."

"Thank you," I told her.

She said, "By the way, I think your daughter might have the sight. For your sake, I hope not."

Madame Zelda took my hands into her veiny ones. She

said, "I hope I don't see you again. I hope you can let the boy get some rest."

"I'm trying," I said.

"You try harder, and never, sweet girl, never name a child after a gypsy fortune-teller, even if she is legendary."

When I exited the tent, Betty and Zelda were waiting for me. Zelda said, "What did the witch lady want?"

"Oh, she's no witch, honey. She's the one and only legendary Madame Zelda, a gypsy fortune-teller."

Betty said, "What was that about?"

"It's a long story."

We rode the Ferris wheel, Zelda between us. We rode the Tilt-A-Whirl, Zelda on the inside. I was in the middle holding on to her, telling her that it was just this thing called centrifugal force. "Don't be scared."

Betty said, "And chaos. Every ride is different depending on the number and weight of the riders."

I shook my head at Betty.

She said, "That's why it's my favorite."

Zelda said, "Mine too. Because of chaos."

I wondered how I was going to stop living my lie. I knew where it would have to start. I would have to tell Betty the truth about who I was and how I felt. From there, I would have to make it clear that whatever I did had to be in the best interest of Zelda. I could divorce Jacob. I could move back to Maryville. Eventually, Betty and I could be together. We could be roommates. No one had to know the truth about us, if there could be an us, if she would love me how I loved her.

After riding the Tilt-A-Whirl a dizzying ten times, Zelda and I pinned against Betty as our car swung, we petted the donkeys and rabbits. We noshed hot dogs and French fries. By the time we walked back to Betty's car, Zelda was unconscious. Betty carried her. "Tonight was a great night," she said.

"Unforgettable." Betty laid Zelda in the back seat and I climbed in beside her. As Betty started the engine, I said, "Do you think we can come to your house?"

"How come?"

"Jacob's out of town, and I want to talk." If I didn't tell Betty the truth now, I didn't know when I would tell her, if I'd ever tell her. It wasn't going to get easier.

"Okay."

"I'll tell you about Madame Zelda."

Betty's house was only five miles from the fairgrounds. She parked in the alleyway behind her apartment. My palms were sweating. I picked Zelda up and carried her upstairs to Betty's apartment. It had parquet floors and one exposed brick wall. Four windows fronted the street. They were draped with blue curtains. I set Zelda down on the sofa, covering her with an afghan, and wiped my palms down the front of my jeans before blurting, "I'm in love with you. I'm not who you think I am."

"What?" Betty said.

"I'm in love with you."

"What the fuck are you talking about, Gloria? First, you're magically aligned with bees. Then, your daughter's namesake is a gypsy who happens to be at the town carnival, and now, you're telling me that you're in love with me. Are you taking hallucinogens?"

Before I could respond, she said, "And for the record, there's no way that that wind picked Zelda up and carried her to that tent. I wouldn't be surprised if your gypsy fortune-teller didn't grab her."

"I don't know where to start," I said.

"The beginning is always a good place. I don't know what's going on with you lately."

"I'm sorry." Betty was understandably frustrated.

"Do you want a drink?"

"Yes."

Betty got down two glasses and poured some wine. She handed me a glass. "So what's going on? And be honest. Please."

"Well," I started, "you know the real me. I'm in love with you. I have no doubts about that. I've been in love with you for years, and yes, my daughter is named after a fortune-teller. Honeybees are my spirit animal, and I'm really tired of living a lie."

"Slow down."

"I never loved Jacob. I tried to love him. I've been trying to be what other people want me to be, what I thought I needed to be. I'm so sorry, and I was going to tell you the whole truth, and then I got pregnant, and I didn't know what the fuck to do. I'm so sorry, Betty."

We stood at the bar separating the kitchen from the living room. Betty topped off our glasses. "I'm speechless," she said.

"That never happens."

"No joke, Gloria."

I said, "Remember that first day you came over with your coconut cookies and we listened to Carole King?"

"Yes."

"And remember the time I kissed you?"

"Of course. I won't forget that."

"I was in love with you then. I've loved you since the first day we met, Betty."

"You never said that you liked women or that you'd ever liked women."

"I was scared."

"Did you used to date old gypsy fortune-tellers? Is that what that was about?"

"She's a little old for me." I sipped from my glass. "The Gloria you don't know has always been attracted to women. She had her first and only girlfriend when she was sixteen. She was in love with her." I got goosebumps. There was so much to explain, so much to reveal. "Her name was Isabel, but she broke up with Gloria. She was only experimenting.

"After Isabel left, Gloria was really sad and agreed to be admitted to a terrible place called the Belmont Institute where she could be 'cured' of her homosexuality." My voice quivered.

"I'm talking about myself in third person. Ugh, this is hard. I never talk about this."

"You've said plenty. I really don't know how I'm supposed to respond. You've been lying to me."

I looked at Betty's wine-stained lips. "But I have to explain. I have to stop hiding. When I was at the institute, I met this boy, this amazing boy, who assured me that there was nothing wrong with me. We were born how we were born. We shouldn't have to feel guilty or apologize for who we were. I loved him. He made me fight for who I was, for what I believed." Betty came to my side of the bar and, setting her glass down, wrapped her arms around me. She pressed her lips to my head, and I looked up to see her. "I loved him so much."

Betty said, "You and Zelda are my world. Have you noticed that I'm always around? I'm not going anywhere. Whatever happens, I'll always be here for you."

We moved to the sofa opposite where Zelda slept. Betty tucked her feet up under her legs. "So, what happened to your friend?"

I took a deep breath. "He died." Then, I didn't say anything for a minute. I couldn't. "But before he died, we lived. He tried to live, anyway. We met Madame Zelda on Coney Island, and she didn't see his fortune."

"What was his name?"

"He's with the bees," I said. "Somehow. That first time I

met Madame Zelda, she said that the bees carried messages between worlds. They've always followed me. He's with them. He comes to me in dreams. He comes to her in dreams."

"What's his name?"

I didn't want to say it. I didn't want to break down. I said, "I'm going to leave Jacob."

"Are you sure?"

"I never should've married him, except if I hadn't, I never would've had Zelda. I wouldn't have met you. Do you know that Sheff used to say that if he and I ever had children, we'd have the most beautiful children in the world? And I did . . . We did."

Betty said, "You said his name. His name was Sheff?"

"His name was Sheffield Schoeffler, and I loved him very much." Tears began to fall. They were the kind of tears that fall without sound; the kind that fall without embarrassment, apology, or thought; the kind that should never be wiped away. "Sheff sent Madame Zelda to the carnival tonight to remind me of what's so apparent. It's time for me to fly."

"What are you going to tell Jacob? What are you going to say?"

"I don't know. I can't tell him the truth. I mean, I can't tell him that I'm in love with you. He'd take Zelda. I'm going to tell him that I don't love him. I'm going to tell him that I'm leaving."

"Are you really in love with me?"

"I'm certain."

Betty set down her wineglass, and we kissed. I didn't kiss her. She didn't kiss me. We kissed. She said, "No one's going to take Zelda from you."

"No. You're right. I won't let them."

31

We slept over at Betty's. I dreamed of Sheff sitting on the velveteen sofa of the Hotel Chelsea. He was smiling and waving and looking so fine, I didn't think he knew he was in my dream. I woke on the sofa with Zelda's fingers in my hair. "I had a sleepover at Aunt Betty's."

"It looks like you have chocolate on your face."

"Aunt Betty gave me some cake before she went downstairs to work. She didn't want to wake you. I said I'd watch you."

"Thanks for watching me." The phone rang. I wasn't going to pick it up. It was Betty's home phone. She had another phone downstairs in the restaurant. I knew that when Betty got off work at two, she'd drive me and Zelda home. Until then, I thought we could stroll around town, get a bite at the restaurant, and go to the library. They had a story time at twelve thirty on Saturdays. There was an antique store on First Street that had fun costume jewelry. I went down the hall to brush my teeth. The phone finally stopped ringing, but then immediately started again. Zelda said, "I can get it."

"No, it's Betty's phone, honey."

I brushed my teeth. The phone was still ringing. I went to the kitchen, worried that it might have something to do with Betty's mother, and picked up. "Hello."

"Gloria?"

"This is she."

"It's me. What are you doing at Betty's? Why didn't you come home?"

"We spent the night after the carnival. It was late."

Jacob said, "I was worried sick."

"You said that you were staying in Raleigh."

"I said that I *might* stay in Raleigh."

"Okay, but you always stay overnight in Raleigh."

"I'm coming to get you."

"Don't do that." I poured a cup of coffee. "I let Oscar out before we went to the carnival. He should be fine. We're fine. I think I'm going to take Zelda to the library. Betty can drive us home when she gets off at two. I left enough food for Oscar. The dog should be fine."

"I don't care about Oscar. I had a real shit night, and I want my family at home." He hung up.

I looked at Zelda. "Daddy will be here in a minute. Let's go say bye to Aunt Betty."

"I want to go to the library."

"I know, sweetheart, but we can go on Monday."

"When's Monday?"

"Not too far from now." I took her hand. She was still wearing her red cowboy boots, her blonde curls tangled at the nape of her neck. We headed downstairs. From the sidewalk, I looked through the plate glass window embossed *Betty's Bakery.* The letters were frosty. I saw Betty smiling behind the counter. Every table was full. She was such a joyful person, and she loved me. It was hard to fathom that I could be so fortunate. I pushed the door open and a bell jingled. She looked up. "Good morning," she said.

"Hi," I said meekly. She put her hands on my shoulders and smiled.

"What can I get you two for breakfast?"

"I'd like more cake," Zelda said.

"I guessed that."

I said, "No more cake, honey." To Betty, I said, "Jacob's on his way to get us."

"I thought he was in Raleigh."

"So did I."

"Don't go," she said. "Stay and have breakfast."

"I can't do that. You know that." Just then, his truck pulled up outside.

"We have to go," I said.

"What are you going to do?"

"I'm going to do what we talked about. I'm going to tell him that it's over."

"Call me, okay. I'll be home after two. Or you can call here." She leaned in and squeezed me tight. Zelda squeezed her leg. Jacob honked the horn.

As we left the restaurant, Jacob was getting out of the truck. He opened the passenger-side door and lifted Zelda up. It was a blustery, crisp day, blue as far as I could see. He took hold of my face and kissed me. "I got home around four this morning, and I was lonely for my girls."

"That's nice." I felt like I was going to be physically sick. Why had he suddenly changed his plans and come home from Raleigh? As I climbed into the truck, I looked back at Betty. She was watching us through the plate glass window.

He said, "So tell me about the fair."

I rolled my window down.

Zelda said, "There was an old witch lady there in a big tent."

"What else?"

"They had cotton candy and a pumpkin patch. Mommy, where's my pumpkin?"

"I think we left it at Betty's."

"We need to get it. I want to sleep with him."

As we pulled up to the house, Oscar came out to greet us. He licked Zelda, and she squealed.

Jacob said, "What do you have planned for today? I miss spending time with you."

"I'm going to get cleaned up," I said, "then work in the garden."

He said, "I can help you get cleaned up. I could wash your back."

I couldn't remember the last time we'd been intimate. "That's okay," I said. "I'm good."

He followed me upstairs, his boots tromping. "I'm sorry that I've been gone so much with work."

"That's okay."

I heard Zelda running up behind us. "Daddy," she said, "you can play dolls with me."

"I'm going to play with Mommy today."

"I'll play too," she said.

I went into the bathroom and locked the door. I could hear Zelda telling Jacob about her doll collection. *I have to get out of here. I have to take Zelda and go away, maybe to Maryville for a while, someplace where we'll be safe.* I towel-dried my hair and looked in the mirror. For a second, I thought I saw Sheff looking back. I touched the glass. "I'm strong," I said, my fingers lingering where I'd seen his face in my own.

As I was getting dressed, Jacob called up from the kitchen, "I made breakfast. Are you hungry?"

Zelda ran upstairs. "Daddy made eggs."

We sat at the kitchen table, the three of us, eating fried eggs and bacon. Jacob said, "Aren't you impressed? I'm home on a Saturday, and I made breakfast!"

"Sure." I didn't know what to say. *Why today? You're never home on weekends.* After breakfast, he trailed me to the shed. I got a trowel. He picked one up. "We're going to have a great

279

day," he said. I pulled my hair back in a kerchief and shrugged.
I didn't know him, or maybe the bigger problem was that I *did*
know him. We went to the flower bed bordering the picket
fence. I dug the weeds out around the chrysanthemums and
deadheaded some of them. I noticed a few bees by one of the
flowers and stopped digging.

Jacob thrust his trowel into the dirt, back and forth, ac-
complishing nothing. "Look, Gloria," he said, jabbing his
trowel uselessly, "I'll be close to home from here on out. I love
you and Zelda so much."

"What happened in Raleigh that made you drive home in
the middle of the night?"

"Can't a man love his family without getting the third degree? Jesus Christ!"

"Of course."

Around five o'clock, Early Bird pulled up with a twelve-
pack of beer. He and Jacob retired to the workshop. I knew
that they'd drink the whole thing and anything else Jacob had
stashed out there. Then, tomorrow, he'd spend all day at the
flea market. That would be my chance to get away. I'd leave
a note. I'd borrow money from my parents and get a lawyer.
I was done. I understood what Sheff was telling me, the same
thing I'd been telling myself. I deserved to be happy.

I went to the shed and put my gardening gloves and trowel
up. I pulled the kerchief from my hair and shook out my curls.
I remembered when the bees had swallowed me. I didn't know
if it had been real, but it had seemed real. It had always seemed

that they meant to protect me, and soon they'd hibernate. Maybe by the time they returned in the spring, I would be free.

I went to the kitchen and washed my hands. Zelda got on her step stool and washed hers. She said, "All clean."

"Are you ever going to take off that dress?" I asked.

"Maybe when I get a kitten."

"Funny."

"I know."

"But what about when you take a bath?"

"Maybe then."

She followed me upstairs. "It's time to read to Oscar," she said. The dog ran after her.

I pulled my red suitcase out from under the bed and popped the silver latch. The lining was a silky beige fabric decorated with red rain boots. It smelled like the Hotel Chelsea, like I'd boxed my time there. It was like Pandora's box now unleashed in Greeley. I was going to live how Sheff had said we'd live, just how we pleased. I was going to be with Betty. I was going to stop walking on eggshells. I could do this: Uncle Eddie knew I could do it. My parents knew. Sheff knew. I packed my underwear, clothes (I didn't have much), and my copy of *The Catcher in the Rye* in my suitcase. I admired the blue dress Betty had bought me. Then, I smiled, imagining waking up to Betty every morning. I opened my cardboard jewelry box, the kind with the ballerina who dances, and pulled out the Madame Zelda handbill I'd found at the Jersey Shore. I stuffed it down beside the dress. Tomorrow, I'd pack Zelda's things. As long as she had her fancy dress, nothing else really mattered. I latched the suitcase just as Zelda and Oscar bounded into the room.

"Are we going on a trip? Are we flying on an airplane?"

"Nope. We're not going anywhere." I slid the suitcase back under the bed.

She said, "When the Berenstain Bears went on a trip, they packed a brown suitcase."

I heard the kitchen door open. "Gloria!"

"I'm upstairs."

"What's for dinner?"

Zelda ran downstairs. "Mommy has a red suitcase. The Berenstain Bears have a brown one." I followed after her.

"What do you want for dinner?" I asked.

"What suitcase?" Jacob asked.

"Mommy has a red suitcase."

Jacob tromped upstairs. Zelda ran after and I followed. "I can make anything for dinner. What do you feel like? Do you want sloppy joes?"

Jacob scanned the bedroom. "Are you going somewhere?"

I closed my eyes for a second. Very softly, I said, "I'm not going anywhere."

"Where's your suitcase?" Jacob crouched down and looked under the bed.

"Right where it always is," I said.

He pulled it out, lifting it onto the bed. "Except it doesn't feel empty."

"Sometimes, I just store stuff in there."

He unlatched it. "Strange. You packed the same clothes you always wear, including this stupid dress. Where are you ever going to wear this?" He threw it on the floor. "And you packed your stupid book." He flung it to the dresser. He rubbed his chin like Rodin's *The Thinker*. "So where are you going?"

Zelda said, "She's not going anywhere."

Jacob said, "Go play in your room. Daddy needs to talk to Mommy alone. And you're exactly right. She's not going anywhere."

Zelda was still in her fancy dress. She shook her head. "I'm staying with Mommy."

He said, "Go! Now!"

She burst into tears.

"Don't yell at Zelda," I said.

Jacob pulled the rest of my clothes from the suitcase and threw them on the floor.

"I thought you weren't going anywhere."

This wasn't ever going to be quiet or easy—the leaving. No matter how I left, sneaking out while he was at work, leaving a note, calling him on the telephone, he'd come after me. Very gently, I said, "We're leaving."

He laughed, his eyes sharklike. "You actually think that that's going to happen."

"I can't be here anymore. I can't do this anymore."

"For better or for worse, Gloria." He turned to Zelda. "Go

to your room!" When she didn't move, he picked her up, toting her down the hall. She kicked her feet, her boots striking his thighs. "Goddamn it!"

"Put Zelda down."

She flailed in his grasp.

I followed him into her room, where he tossed her on her bed and grabbed my arm. "Come with me." He pulled Zelda's door shut. From the hallway, I heard her crying.

"Let me go." I was going to get my daughter and call Betty to come get us, take Jacob's stupid truck, or leave on foot. I tried to pry his hand off my arm. He flung me into the wall. "Just let us go," I said. He pressed my face to the wall, pinning my arm behind me. "We're leaving."

"But you're not," he said. "I know that everything's been all fucked up because I haven't been around. I know that I haven't been a good husband, but that's going to change. I had some shit I had to deal with." I thought of Darlene. I'd heard the rumors, but as far as I'd been concerned, Darlene was doing us a favor. He said, "I'm going to start taking care of you again." I felt his breath on my neck. He spun me around, pressing his lips to mine, and I bit him.

"Fuck you, Gloria!" He flung me harder against the wall before grabbing me around the waist. "You want to play rough? Is that how you want to do this? You've been running wild like an untamed horse."

"I want to go."

I heard Zelda's door open. Jacob pinned both arms to my

side, forcing me down the hall. Zelda grabbed hold of his thigh. "Put Mommy down."

"Please stop, Jacob." I tried to speak calmly. Then, Oscar started barking. He showed Jacob his teeth. Zelda screamed, and Jacob kicked Oscar in the ribs. "Please." I writhed, kicking my legs, my feet braced against the wall.

He said, "Why do you have to do this shit to me, to make me look like the bad guy? You're the bad guy, Gloria." Zelda was still screaming. Jacob forced me into the bathroom. He screamed at Zelda. "Go to your room!"

I said, "Please listen to Daddy." I didn't want her to see whatever was about to happen.

"But, Mommy . . ."

"Mommy's okay. Go on now."

Jacob said, "That's more like it."

As Zelda left, I heard Oscar follow. I said to Jacob, "Can we please just start over?"

He set me down. "That's all I want. All I want is for everything to be good with us."

I ventured, "Maybe we just need a little time apart."

"That's the last fucking thing we need. That's how we've been living. Don't think I take my wedding vows lightly. You love me. You're my wife. Take off your fucking clothes."

"I don't want to do that."

"I don't give a shit, Gloria."

I tried to rush past him, but he caught me at the waist and flung me back. My calves struck the bathtub while the rest of me kept going, my head smacking the wall before I dropped in a heap. He said, "You're not going to leave me. I'm going to give you what you've been missing." He grabbed me by my hair and slugged my jaw. The left side of my face was numb. I smelled the beer on his breath. He dragged me along the floor so that my head was between the sink base and the commode. Then, he started unbuttoning my pants. He was breathing heavily. "I'm the man of the house!" I tried to get up, but he knocked my head against the floor. "Goddamn it, Gloria."

I heard the door open. *Zelda.* "Stop it, Daddy! Leave Mommy alone!"

"Go to your room, goddamn it."

"Daddy, stop it!" She was crying hard, and there was nothing I could do. I fought, but the harder I fought, the harder he gripped my throat, his thumb pressing against my windpipe. Then, I heard them. Before I saw them, I heard them. They swarmed into the bathroom, gathering where the plaster hung in sheets from the ceiling. I couldn't breathe. I tried to unhinge Jacob's grip, but he was too strong. He was bearing down, his thighs like a vise at my waist. I knew Zelda was there. She could see. *Please don't see. Please make it stop. Please.* He slammed the back of my head into the bathroom tile. I heard the bees' hum grow louder. Zelda screaming, "Get off, Mommy!" Oscar barking. I was going to die. I searched with my hands for something to use as a weapon. I dug at the grout until a piece of old tile broke loose. I used everything I had to shoot it up into his neck.

"Why do you . . . ? Why . . . ?" he said, and then his voice gurgled, the bees descending, a yellow and black swirling mass, blood pouring warm from Jacob's neck. The bees covered his face, their stingers punctured his skin. They fell like yellow and black rain to my face and chest, and I was falling too, through the cracked floor into blackness, when I heard a familiar voice, Sheff's: "I've got you, Gloria. I've always got you."

32

I woke in a white room, white walls, white ceiling, white bedcovers, white window wide-open, fat bumblebees passing through; Betty in a white dress, a Florence Nightingale walking toward me.

"Where am I?"

"She's talking."

I reached for her hand. Then I dropped down through a green canopy of trees into a hollowed-out stump with a million yellow cells, sweet golden legs piling and packing nectar into hexagonal cells. I was a part of this: *Honeybees protect themselves by stinging intruders.*

I woke to the name Zelda: a woman with long fingers, bejeweled, picking, piling, sorting, dealing cards. She showed me her hand, a full house, three queens and a pair of aces, and then Betty was holding my hands. I heard the words *head trauma* and *stay with me* before I fell again, this time into the bathroom. Jacob's hands at my throat. *You're my fucking wife.*

I don't want to be your wife. I want to go. I have to go. Golden dust fell from the ceiling. The dust turned to bees. "We've got you." I heard my mother's voice. "Why don't you take Zelda to the snack machine?"

Betty said, "I'll tell the nurse she's awake."

"I need you." I reached for Zelda, but she was too far away. *Zelda.* I fell again, this time into a whiteness like salt. *Don't let Jacob take my baby.* The salt thinned into light. It swallowed everything.

"Her pupils are responding."

"You're okay." It was my mother's voice.

"I think I'm dead."

There was a woman with red hair holding a flashlight. "I'm Nurse Mary. How are you feeling today?"

I didn't answer.

I saw my mother and reached for her. She didn't disappear. I didn't fall. I held on. She kissed my forehead. "You gave us a scare."

"Where's Sheff? He was with me."

My mother smiled sympathetically. "She's still disoriented."

"It'll pass. It'll take time."

"We were going to have the most beautiful children in the world."

My mother said, "Can you get Zelda?" My father stood at the foot of the bed.

"Where am I?"

"You're in the hospital."

"Daddy." He came closer, and I saw his one hand, the bones pointing in the wrong direction. I didn't remember it looking so terrible. I said, "There's something wrong with me."

My father said, "You have a brain injury, Gloria, but you're going to be all right."

"Where's Zelda?"

"I'll get her."

My father left and my mother sat at my side. "How long have I been here?"

"Three weeks."

"Am I really going to be okay?"

"You are." She kissed my forehead, and I reached up to feel my head. My hair was gone.

Then, Betty came in holding Zelda's hand. Zelda charged the bed, climbing up. "My baby," I said. "I missed you." My mother moved my IV line out of her way.

"I'm careful," Zelda said. She wore a bright pink dress and black tap shoes. "Pa Pa got me the shoes with the clickers that *tap tap*." She climbed down to show me her dance routine just as a doctor came into the room. He showed me his nametag.

"I'm Dr. Fisher," he said. "Good morning, Gloria. Do you know where you are this morning?"

"A hospital."

"Who's the president of the United States?"

"Jimmy Carter, the last I knew anyway."

"Can you name the days of the week for me?"

I named them.

"What's the last thing you remember?"

I looked at Zelda. "I . . ."

"Daddy went to heaven with the angels," Zelda said. "He's happy there."

Everyone looked at me. I nodded. I had nothing to add. The doctor finished his examination and said, "You look good today."

"Thank you."

He explained that I'd suffered an acute head trauma. It'd been touch and go for a while. He never knew how these things would play out. There'd been fluid on my brain and they'd had to drain it off, but as far as he could tell, I was out of the woods. They would keep me in the hospital for a while longer. See how I did. "I'll see you in the morning," he said, and then he was gone.

Later that evening, after Betty and Zelda had gone home, I sat with my parents. The television was on low, and it was dark outside my window. I whispered to my mother, "The beehive killed him. It was terrifying, and they died, all the bees died."

My mother said, "What hive, sweetheart? There was no beehive. It was self-defense."

33

Denouement

HOME WASN'T MARYVILLE, AND IT certainly wasn't the house on Priddy Lane. Home was with my daughter and with the woman I loved in the two-bedroom apartment above her bakery. Home was the smell of fresh-baked bread and pungent cheese. Home was the sound of Zelda's footie pajamas slapping the floor, her laughter. Home was the sound of Oscar's nails on the steps, sliding across the parquet flooring as he chased down a tennis ball. Home was singing along to the Rolling Stones' "I Can't Get No Satisfaction," and dancing to the music of Donna Summer. Home was the three of us squeezed into one bathroom, Zelda standing on the toilet as we brushed our teeth. Like a good cake, home had many layers. More than anything, home was not feeling guilty or afraid.

For Christmas, my mother bought me a typewriter. She said, "I remember that you used to like to write stories."

For weeks, I eyed it on my dresser, afraid of what might come out when I finally put my fingers to the keys. Every night after Zelda and Betty were asleep, I talked to Sheff, telling him about my life. "I'm doing it. Really living. I'm happy and in love." He came to me in dreams, but I was no longer running, being chased, or chasing after something unattainable. Sheff came and he went, and when he came, I welcomed him. He crouched in the darkest recesses of the Belmont ballroom, telling me that he was going to go to Chelsea to see Sal Mineo. I could meet him there. He sat on the Chelsea's velveteen sofa, holding his copy of *Howl*, waiting for Allen Ginsberg to return. Next time, he'd find the words to talk to him. He rowed across Turtle Pond, bees flying out from his blond hair. I even saw him on a bus bound for California. He was in all the places we'd been and in the places where we were meant to go. Most often, I dreamed of him sitting in Madame Zelda's tent on Coney Island. The mermaid woman was there too. So were the bees. He was still asking for that fortune.

On Saturday afternoons, Zelda and I went with Betty to the nursing home to see her mother, whose name was Victoria. Even when she didn't remember who Betty was, she always seemed to know Zelda. She called her "my queen bee," and it made me think that maybe Madame Zelda had been right about my Zelda. Maybe she did have some special sight. Maybe she *was* the queen bee.

In the spring, Betty and I planted a flower and herb garden. The bees returned, building a hive in a hollowed-out stump, and we watched with wonder as they constructed their home. They flew flower to flower, collecting nectar and pollen and returning to the hive.

Sometimes Betty and I forgot that we weren't supposed to show affection in public. We held hands or looked at each other lovingly. Once, we kissed in public. We heard the rumors that the two lesbians were raising a soon-to-be lesbian. "That's what happens when those kind try to be parents. It's unnatural." Betty and I chose to ignore them. People still came to the bakery for bread and cakes. They came to the restaurant for breakfast and lunch. Seeing two lesbians living together was a much-needed addition to the Greeley gossip mill.

It was a sunny fall day before I finally summoned the courage to sit down at the typewritter, my fingers on the keys. *His name was Sheffield Schoeffler. I met him in the fall of 1965 at the Belmont Institute. I loved him.*

Acknowledgments

WHEN I WAS SIXTEEN, I met a group of boys on vacation in the Outer Banks of North Carolina. One of them confessed to me and my friend that he was gay. He had just graduated from high school, he had a core group of best friends he'd known all his life, and none of them knew that he was gay. He said, "If they ever found out, they wouldn't like me. They'd be afraid of me." He told my friend and I that if he could be "straight," he would be. He cried. He was the saddest boy I'd ever met, and he's remained with me for all these years. I brought him back to life in Sheffield Schoeffler. I like to think that the boy from the beach went off to college and found the strength to live true to himself. I like to think that he told his friends about his sexuality, and that they were kinder and wiser than he knew, that they accepted him for who he was. This novel is for every boy like him. It's for every child growing up in a world that doesn't seem to want them.

Thank you to my readers: Maggie Bryson, Loretta Sanders, Lisa Sharp, Danny Stone, and Christopher Young-Stone. Thank you, Mom, for your unconditional love, the Catholic stories of your childhood, and for the stories about Mary Martin's *Peter Pan. I won't grow up.* Thank you to my friends and family for your support during the dark days, when the scenes and characters were overwhelming. Thank you to my dancing compadres at the Y for the freedom to cut loose off the page, and thank you to my agent of ten years, Michelle Brower, for your candor and wisdom.

This book has a plethora of artistic influences, and I would feel remiss if I didn't mention some of them: Elizabeth Bishop (poet), David Bowie (singer, songwriter, actor), Marlene Dietrich (actress, singer), Allen Ginsberg (poet), Ernest Hemingway (novelist), Grace Kelly (actress and princess), Jack Kerouac (novelist), Carole King (singer, songwriter), Mary Martin (actress), Sal Mineo (actor), J. D. Salinger (novelist), Frank Sinatra (actor, singer, songwriter), Bessie Smith (singer, songwriter, actress), and Elizabeth Taylor (actress, activist). I am indebted to the *British Journal of Psychiatry*'s article, "Treatments of homosexuality in Britain since the 1950s—an oral history: the experience of patients," by Glenn Smith, Annie Bartlett, and Michael King (2004, Feb. 21), where I first read about the use of apomorphine in aversion therapy to "treat" homosexuality.

About the Author

MICHELE YOUNG-STONE is also the author of two previous novels, *Above Us Only Sky* and *The Handbook for Lightning Strike Survivors*. She is at work on a fourth and fifth. Michele lives in the Outer Banks of North Carolina with her husband and son.

Simon & Schuster Paperbacks
Reading Group Guide

Lost in the Beehive

This reading group guide for Lost in the Beehive *includes an
introduction, discussion questions, and ideas for enhancing your
book club. The suggested questions are intended to help your reading group find new and interesting angles and topics for your discussion. We hope that these ideas will enrich your conversation and
increase your enjoyment of the book.*

Introduction

For nearly her entire life, Gloria Ricci has been followed by bees. They're there when her mother loses twin children, when she first meets a neighborhood girl named Isabel, who brings out feelings in her that she thinks she shouldn't have, and when her parents, desperate to "help" her, bring her to the Belmont Institute, whose glossy brochures promise healing and peace. She tells no one, but their hum follows her as she struggles to survive against the institute's cold and damaging methods, as she meets an outspoken and unapologetic fellow patient named Sheffield Schoeffler, and as they run away, toward the freewheeling and accepting glow of 1960s Greenwich Village, where they create their own kind of family among the artists and wanderers who frequent the jazz bars and side streets.

As Gloria tries to outrun her past, experiencing profound love—and loss—and encountering a host of unlikely characters from her Uncle Eddie, a hard-drinking former boyfriend of her mother's, to Madame Zelda, a Coney Island fortune-teller, and Jacob, the man she eventually marries, whose dark side threatens to bring disaster, the bees remain. It's only when she needs them most that Gloria discovers why they're there. Moving from the suburbs of New Jersey to the streets of New York to the swamps of North Carolina and back again, *Lost in the Beehive* is a touching novel about the moments that teach us, the places that shape us, and the people who change us.

Topics and Questions for Discussion

1. This novel is told in three parts, each exploring a distinct phase in Gloria's coming-of-age journey, from her burgeoning adolescence to her tumultuous marriage to her unexpected motherhood. Which part resonated with you the most, and why?

2. When we first meet Gloria, she's heartsick, tortured by the loss of her first love. In what way(s) is this heartbreak a formative experience for her? Do you remember your first love (or your first heartbreak), and how can you relate to Gloria's experience?

3. Gloria endures an especially cruel method of therapy at the Belmont Institute that requires her to repeat detailed accounts of her "sins." Describe your reaction to these painful scenes. Did you identify a glimmer of good intentions in Mrs. Dupree and the Belmont staff?

4. After returning home from Belmont, Gloria decides to take charge of her destiny by running away to join Sheff in Chelsea, saying, "I was simply determined to live my life on my own terms" (page 60). At what moments in the novel does she live up to this edict, and when does she veer off course? At what moments does she *think* she's living life on her own terms, when it may be clear to the reader that she's not?

5. Discuss the unique bond between Gloria and Sheff, especially in terms of the acceptance and support that these damaged characters provide one another.

6. What was your reaction to the horrific reality of Sheff's "therapy" as described on page 100? Were you surprised by the physical torture that Sheff endured, and how did this pivotal revelation affect your reaction to Sheff's ultimate fate?

7. On page 53, Sheff says, "It's no good being alive if you don't get to live." Knowing what we do of Sheff's tragic end, reflect on these powerful words. Furthermore, how does Sheff's philosophy on life impact Gloria's own path?

8. During Gloria's courtship and early marriage to Jacob, she reflects, "I didn't love him. Of course not, but I was participating, joining the land of the living" (page 147). Have there been moments in your own life when you've faked your way through an experience just to keep up appearances or because it seemed the path of least resistance?

9. Gloria falls victim to the fallacy of the American Dream in the early years of her marriage to Jacob: "I felt like I was really succeeding, living that American dream—even the picket fence" (page 193). But as Gloria learns, there's danger (and misery) in basing one's perception of success or happiness on this socially constructed image. Discuss

Gloria's inner turmoil at this stage in her life; what are her options as a queer woman at this time in history? Would you have behaved any differently in her shoes?

10. Gloria's relationship with her parents—especially her mother—evolves significantly over the course of the novel. In the opening chapters, Gloria realizes that she's "been taking care of [her]self" (page 46) and resents her parents' decision to send her to the Belmont Institute in an attempt to "fix" her. By the novel's end, her parents have become a loving support system for her, particularly in the wake of her mother's own healing journey. Did you find this to be a realistic portrayal of a changing parent-child dynamic? Why, or why not?

11. Discuss Jacob's character. What was your first impression of him? Overall, do you consider him a villain, or were there redeeming moments in Jacob's life?

12. The night that Gloria feels her baby kick for the first time, she dreams of the bees: "They were buzzing through the pines behind my parents' house. I trailed them. They were moving faster and faster, and I was chasing, but we ran a loop back to my parents' house. I could never catch up" (page 243). Dissect the imagery presented in this dream as it relates to Gloria's struggles at this particular stage in her life's journey.

13. Discuss Betty's character. How does she help Gloria throughout the novel? Did you predict the evolution of their relationship?

14. Toward the end of the novel, Gloria reunites with Madame Zelda, who shares a message from Sheff: "The boy wants you to know that you have to honor who you are. Don't let anyone turn you into someone you aren't, Gloria. He says that Holden somebody didn't become a phony" (page 267). Why do these words have such a dramatic impact on Gloria?

15. Bee stings come at dark moments in Gloria's life: for example, the death of her mother's twins and the moment when she says, "I do," and yet, as the novel progresses, the bees appear to swarm around her at times when she needs support, bringing her a sense of comfort. What do you interpret to be their purpose in Gloria's life?

16. Contemplate the Ernest Hemingway quote that opens Part One of the novel. What are Gloria's "broken places"? By novel's end, is she strong in the "broken places"?

17. How would Gloria's life be different if she came of age today? Think about your own coming-of-age. Were LGBT young people accepted?

Enhance Your Book Club

1. The classic novel *The Catcher in the Rye* is cited multiple times throughout this book. Read J.D. Salinger's beloved masterpiece in tandem with *Lost in the Beehive*, and compare Holden's 1950s coming-of-age journey to Gloria's own '70s-set story. Which of their experiences are comparable, and which diverge? Which elements of both narratives reflect universal truths about the pain—and triumphs—of adolescence?

2. The popular radio program, *This American Life*, hosted by Ira Glass, shares a true story about conversion therapy in Act Three of Episode 462. The episode (which is titled "Own Worst Enemy") is available online at thisamericanlife.org/radio-archives/episode/462/own -worst-enemy. Listen to Act Three, "Just As I Am," and discuss the story of John Smid and love in action as it relates to the journeys of Gloria and Sheff.

3. Betty and her bakery bring comfort and stability to Gloria's life during her tumultuous marriage. Ask every member of your book group to bring their favorite baked good—either prepared from scratch or store-bought— that they associate with a sense of comfort. Share your stories as you share your treats!

4. Bees are Gloria's "spirit animal"—what's yours? Have every member of the book group identify his or her spirit animal, and bring a representation of that creature to the discussion to prompt a fun dialogue.